A NOT
SO COZY
CHRISTMAS

HOLT JACOBS MYSTERY - BOOK 4

LILY STIRLING

~ To Rhett ~
Merry Christmas.

CONTENTS

Chapter 1

Was I making the biggest mistake of my life? Don't get me wrong. I've made some monumentally bad decisions, but I've never brought a girl to a family Christmas.

"The roads don't look that bad," Brittany said from beside me.

Apparently my girlfriend thought I was white-knuckling the steering wheel because of the roads. I guess it was a good thing she didn't know how close I was to pulling a U-turn and driving back to the airport.

"Hopefully it doesn't start snowing harder," Britt said.

Hold on.

Brittany was talking about the weather?

Why would Brittany be talking about the weather?

I risked a glance at her, but all I saw in the dark car was her silhouette, with her black hair pulled back in a ponytail. But something was off. Britt sounded like she was chatting with a new acquaintance, not having a relaxed conversation with her boyfriend.

"You're nervous!" My voice was more accusing than I'd meant.

"So are you," she said, but her voice had the practiced calm of a full-time paramedic.

"Sure, I'm nervous," I said. "I'm driving through Montana mountains while it's snowing, at night, and the speed limit's eighty miles an hour."

"The road is straight. The nighttime speed limit is sixty-five—you're driving fifty. And it's just a few snowflakes."

"Uh…" I had to fight a grin. I should probably be irritated at being put in my place, yet I was delighted. Still, for Britt to be talking like that, she had to be pretty nervous.

I decided to be more supportive. I reached over to her side of the car, but all I ended up touching was her large winter coat. "It'll be fine. By the time we get there, Casey's kids will be in bed and it'll just be the six grown-ups."

"Exactly." Brittany gave my arm a quick squeeze—easy for her to do since she wasn't driving. Plus, I wasn't wearing my coat. "That means neither of us has anything to be nervous about."

"Definitely," I said.

"Holt?"

"Yeah?"

"That means you can stop squeezing the steering wheel."

She had a point. Unfortunately, my solution was drumming my fingers on the wheel to keep my grip loose. Finally, when I'd annoyed myself into stopping, I said, "It's not you I'm worried about. I mean"—I ran a hand through my hair—"the last time I was with my whole family, I ended up in an ambulance three different times."

"Well"—Britt's voice was soft—"that wasn't so bad."

My lips rose in the beginning of a smile. "Yeah, my EMT was superhot."

"Holt." Britt's voice was actually serious, and I risked a glance at her. "I'm a paramedic."

"*Paramedic* and *EMT* aren't synonyms?"

Britt laughed. "No. A paramedic has more training."

I frowned. Fifty-four minutes away from bringing my girlfriend to the Jacobs family Christmas and I found out I didn't know what her job was.

"It's not a big deal," she said.

I nodded, but it sounded like a big deal.

Brittany put a hand on my knee. I think she wanted to drive. Not that I was swerving around. I'd even decreased my speed as the snow picked up and began sticking to the road. But I'd resumed white-knuckling the wheel. Problem was, Britt couldn't drive the rental. She hadn't been added to the insurance, not because I was a more experienced winter driver. Her time in Oregon and mine in Seattle barely qualified either of us. No, I was driving because if I'm a passenger on a car trip lasting more than thirty minutes, I usually fall asleep. With me driving, there were two sets of eyes on the road.

Fighting the urge to start drumming on the steering wheel again, I said, "It'll be my parents, who flew in from Australia. I'm the oldest, there's Casey, her husband, Nigel, and their two kids, Baxter and Harper. Then my youngest sister, Juniper, and her husband, Jude."

"I know," Brittany said. "I've vacationed with Juniper and Jude and saw your whole family from a distance when you were in Oregon, and during that trip I talked to your mom a few times."

She'd talked to Mom? Somehow I'd forgotten that. In May, Britt had only spoken to my mother when I'd been a total mess of a human being—which, unfortunately, had happened a lot.

I frowned at the road. "I know you remember them. I'm only saying their names out loud so I don't forget."

"Holt." Brittany's voice was too calm. "What's wrong? I've seen you less nervous confronting killers."

My jaw ticked and my grip on the steering wheel tightened. So much for being a pillar of strength and courage.

"You can tell me," she said, running a hand up and down my biceps before I had a chance to flex. "Are you having second thoughts about bringing me?"

I sighed. My only other real girlfriend had broken up with me because I was too closed off. Problem was, when I speak, my words usually come out wrong. "It's just..." Removing a sweaty hand from the steering wheel, I wiped it on my pants. "It's just..." I shook my head before finally saying the truth. "It's just my family."

Brittany didn't answer. Was she waiting for more?

"The kids are loud. Mom schedules fun and gives me the side-eye if I'm not enjoying myself, and there's just so many people around all the time." I shuddered.

"All right, then" was all Brittany said.

Was it all right? Two years before we started dating, Brittany's hunky coast guard fiancé died. From all accounts, Jeremy was a perfect specimen and was beloved by Britt's mom, who hated me. In addition to Mrs. Asato disliking my overall personality, she blamed me for making Britt move to Seattle—and for her getting kidnapped...which wasn't my fault.

Perfect Jeremy could probably discuss his feelings in a way that grew their relationship. The thought of Britt comparing me to him made my stomach roll.

"Is there anything else?" she asked. "You really don't look well."

I ignored the question. We were approaching a gas station, and I considered stopping. As a general rule I avoid gas station bathrooms—problem was I'd already avoided the airport bathroom.

"Do you need to stop?" I asked, and when Britt said no, I turned right just past the station to leave the highway and bring us one step closer to Mom's Christmas House of Horrors.

Brittany didn't say anything more as we began descending a winding mountain road. The snow was really coming down hard. Large puffy flakes like the kind found in snow globes were coating the road and adding to the layers of snow on the mountains.

For a few seconds the tires trembled as they fought to keep traction before regaining their grip on the road.

My stomach clenched. I wanted to at least make it to the cabin without a car accident. I definitely wasn't looking forward to forty more minutes of this weather. While I couldn't fix the driving conditions, I could try to get on better footing with Britt. "Sorry," I said. "I'm tired, stressed, and ready to be cranky about anything."

"You're tired?" Britt's voice had turned teasing. "You slept the whole flight."

I raised an eyebrow, though Britt couldn't see it in the dark. "The flight wasn't very long."

A few minutes later Brittany said, "It'll be fine." Though I wasn't sure whether she was saying it for her sake or for mine. Then she gasped. "Hold on. Your dad's gift. I set it on the counter because I ran out of tape and never packed it. Holt"—Britt's voice trembled—"we might have to buy him a gift from the gas station."

I'd seen the wrapped book and tossed the present into the suitcase that was nothing but gifts. For a moment I considered pretending Dad's present wasn't in the suitcase. And while, yes, such behavior might earn me a lump of coal from Santa, a part of me still hadn't recovered from the entire Saturday Britt had insisted was necessary to get presents for everyone in my family. In previous years my shopping had all been gift cards or done online. Once Brittany found out we didn't give each other handmade gifts, she insisted we take a day to go to a million different stores to find everyone a perfect gift.

"...can't believe this. Instead of a first edition of *To Kill a Mockingbird*, he'll end up getting a random airport thriller."

"Or *Chicken Soup for Senior Citizens*."

"Are you making jokes right now?" Britt *wasn't* amused.

"No—er, yes. But I packed it. His book's in the presents suitcase."

Britt exhaled. "You're sure?"

"Positive." I forced a grin. "We're all set for a picture-perfect Christmas."

Just then the car began skidding as the tires completely lost traction. "Britt!" I called out—like I was worried she'd disappeared. I moved the steering wheel in the direction my driving instructor had hopefully told me to. It did nothing. We were fishtailing on a mountain road, and I wanted to puke.

On one side there was a guardrail with what I can only assume was a pretty steep decline, while on the other side there was a ditch, large boulders, and a steep incline.

"Britt!" I called again—though I don't know what I was expecting her to do.

The car began swerving in the opposite direction, and I readjusted the wheel.

Suddenly the wheel began trembling as the tires fought to regain a grip on the road. I felt the moment traction was restored and I had full control of the car again. It probably took only a few seconds, but time had stretched out into terrifyingly long milliseconds.

I was about to ask Britt if she was okay, when she shouted, "Stop the car!"

"What happened?" I asked, carefully maneuvering onto the shoulder.

"There was an accident," she said.

What was she talking about? We hadn't hit anything. Was Britt in shock?

I said, "No, we're fine." Then my stomach lurched, and I threw open my car door and dry heaved out the side. When it became clear nothing was coming up, I sat back in my seat and closed the door.

Brittany had grabbed the backpack that had been her personal item on the flight and was digging through it. When I saw her red first aid kit, my stomach gave another flip.

"Are you hurt?"

We'd been buffeted about, but it's not like we'd crashed. Brittany had to be all right.

I clicked the overhead light to see better, and there was Britt taking out a flashlight and covering her ears with a knitted headband.

"What's going on?" I asked.

Brittany's face was overly calm with the paramedic mask she'd spent years perfecting. "There was a car that skidded off the road about where we lost traction." She clicked on the flashlight. "Didn't you see it?"

I shook my head. *Not dying* had been my priority.

"I'm going to go check and see if there are still people in the vehicle."

After I shrugged back into my winter coat, we both got out and began walking along the shoulder, back the way we'd come. I was hoping it was an old wreck, but as we approached, I could tell the tire tracks veering off the road were pretty fresh in the snow. Though even our tire tracks were quickly disappearing under the large snowflakes.

At first all I could make out in the ditch was a dark blob. How had Britt known it was a vehicle? As we grew closer, the glow of Britt's flashlight and my phone's flashlight illuminated a red SUV. There were no lights or sounds coming from the machine. But there were tire tracks showing where the SUV had performed a one-eighty before landing in the drainage ditch between the road and the incline of the mountain.

"Stay here," Britt said as we reached the back of the SUV. "You might not want to see this."

Yeah, like I was going to wait while my girlfriend walked up to a stranger's abandoned car in the mountains in the middle of the night. I've seen enough movies to know that's a bad idea.

Britt rounded the vehicle a couple of steps in front of me. Even in the dim light, horror and confusion played clearly across her face. When I turned the corner, my face must've done the same thing.

Leaning against one of the tires was the slumped silhouette of a man.

I let out a low whistle. With an ice ax jammed through his winter coat and into his heart, I doubt the accident killed him.

Chapter 2

Brittany still checked on the dead man, then looked in the vehicle for other victims—all while I scanned the woods for killers. At the point where I stood next to someone who'd literally been killed by an ax murderer, taking precautions seemed like a good idea.

"Do you have cell reception?" Britt asked as I continued watching the shadows. "I only have one bar."

To my surprise, I did have cell service—in my experience abandoned mountain roads never do.

I called 911. After explaining the death and giving our location, I was informed help would arrive as fast as they could make it in the snow.

Why rush? Not like my girlfriend and I were hanging out by the side of the road with an ax murderer lurking in the shadows. If I was about to star in a low-budget Christmas horror flick, the police would be too late to stop it.

"Did they say when they'd get here?" Britt asked.

I shrugged. "As fast as possible given the road conditions."

"Okay." Britt nodded. "We should go back to the car." From the little scar by her eyebrow, I knew I was her next patient. At this point her priority must be making sure I stayed warm and didn't go into shock.

"Hold on a second," I said. The snow was coming down hard, and the wind was causing drifts. Our shoe prints were beginning to vanish. How much evidence would literally be buried by the time police arrived?

I refocused my phone's flashlight on the scene. The tracks Britt had made to check inside the car were the most obvious, but there were other sets as well. I couldn't say for sure without moving around the vehicle, but besides Brittany's, there appeared to be three separate sets of tracks.

Without moving from my spot, I began videoing to give the police something to go off. From the disturbed snow, you could tell where the victim had been struck before stumbling to his position by the back wheel.

Britt shone her flashlight to help brighten the area as I filmed. When I got a good sample, I put my phone away and said, "Hopefully they won't keep our shoes as evidence."

Britt let out a breath, and I think she was relieved I was myself enough to make a joke. She tugged at my arm, and we headed back to the rental car. A fine layer of snow dusted the car, and I turned on the windshield wipers.

My phone vibrated. It was a text from Mom asking: *Are you driving?*

Her mom-senses were honestly freaky. I decided it would be best to get it over with, so I called. It was no surprise she answered during the first ring.

"We're fine," I said before she could ask the question. "But we came upon a...car accident with a fatality, and we're waiting for the first responders."

While I spoke, the background sounds of other people faded, before disappearing entirely with the click of a door.

"Holt Jacobs, what aren't you telling me?"

I squeezed my eyes shut. Why had I even attempted to give Mom an abridged version of events? "Fine." My voice was more frustrated than intended. "The dead guy didn't die in the crash. He took an ice ax to the heart. There. Happy now?"

There was a masculine cough, and then Dad said, "You're on speaker."

Of course I was.

"Hi, Dad." Clearing my throat, I asked, "Anyone else there?"

"It's just us," Mom said. "The rest of the family is in the living room." Then she added a dash of guilt, saying, "We're all waiting for you."

Could Britt hear our conversation? I glanced at Brittany. Her whole body was rigid. She probably could hear most of it. But I didn't know whether she was amused or upset by the call.

"Mom"—I sighed—"there's nothing we can do about it. The police will want to talk to us."

"Hm" was all Mom said.

"Sorry for messing up your schedule," I grumbled.

Dad gave a half laugh, and I could picture Mom glaring at him so clearly, it felt like I was in the room.

Mom decided to change the subject, instead of delving into her need to control people's lives. "Is Brittany all right? Should we drop off some food?"

"We're fine. The roads are getting bad. No one else should be out."

"This could have been avoided if you'd gotten that earlier flight I suggested," Mom said.

My grip on the phone tightened, and I had to remind myself to speak calmly. "Mom, I told you this was the best flight for our schedules."

"I only meant—" Mom started to say before I interrupted.

"It's better we discovered the accident than a family with a bunch of kids. Britt's a professional. She knew exactly what to do."

Mom didn't respond. Were we in a standoff? When a voice came on the line, it was Dad's. "We'll let you go, so you're ready for the police."

My dad is great.

"All right, thanks."

Still no word from Mom. I refused to feel bad for disagreeing with the self-appointed smartest woman in the world. Still, it was my mother and it was the holidays, so I said, "Love you. Bye."

I didn't hold my breath. I knew Mom would have to say it back since I wasn't one to initiate saying *I love you.*

"Love you, too," Mom and Dad said, not quite in unison.

"Drive safe," Mom added before ending the call.

I glanced at Brittany. It felt weird saying *I love you* in front of her since we'd never said the words to each other. Scrubbing my face with my hands, I said the first thing that came to mind. "I should have used the restroom at the gas station."

When Brittany replied, I couldn't tell if she was amused and it was too dark to see her face. "You could *go* outside."

"In nature?"

"Yes, in nature," Britt said. "I do it all the time on backpacking trips."

I stared at her silhouette. "I'm not *going* out there. First off, it's freezing. And..."

"And?" Britt asked.

"Uhh..." I was really proud of myself when I came up with a second valid point. "And I don't want to contaminate a crime scene."

"Nice save."

"That's what I thought."

When Britt replied, I could hear the smile in her voice. "You wouldn't want a trip to the woods becoming *Exhibit P* in a trial."

Settling back in my seat, I said, "There's already an Amelia's Haven case file with plenty of photos of me in nothing but my boxers. I don't need any new embarrassments added on."

About twenty minutes later the reflection of flashing lights bounced off the snow before a line of emergency vehicles crested the ridge. Brittany was already outside waiting as I fully zipped up my coat and put on gloves.

A group of emergency personnel congregated around us. Brittany didn't need to give her paramedic credentials to have them direct any important questions to her. Basically, I stood there nodding at the right times while wondering if my feet would freeze.

I'd packed snow boots but hadn't worn them for the trip from the airport to the cabin. The choice made sense when I thought I'd be walking in an airport parking lot and on a cabin's sidewalk but one I highly regretted while standing still in inches of snow.

The view had changed drastically once it was illuminated by so many emergency lights. Also, I still needed a restroom, and all the flashing lights were making me dizzy.

Hopefully, I didn't actually sway into Brittany, but there came a moment when she gripped my elbow and asked, "Is there someplace warmer we can talk?"

"Al's gas station is just up the road," one of the officers said.

A second cop nodded. "We'll need copies of his security footage anyway. Come on," he said, leading the way up the row of parked emergency vehicles. "We can take your statements at the gas station."

We followed. While it was nice I wouldn't need to drive back over the icy section of road, I worried my rental would be completely snowed in by the time we returned.

At least there'd be a bathroom—even if it was a gas station bathroom.

"You're doing great," Brittany said as we walked. I turned to look at her, but instead I caught another glimpse of the man impaled by the ice ax.

I nodded. "Uh...thanks."

Usually, Britt and I are on an equal footing, but after emergencies, I get the feeling she's watching me like I'm a science experiment and she's constantly gauging how I'm doing. While I'm happy my girlfriend's both confident and competent, I'd like the opportunity to show her the same support. Yet she's too busy checking on me for me to get a chance to return the favor.

Cop #1 took the shotgun seat as Cop #2 opened the back door for us with a sheepish grin. "Don't take riding in the back personally."

Brittany climbed right in, but I hesitated. Frozen feet were one thing. Being locked in the back of a cop car was something else.

"Holt?" Brittany held out her hand. Sighing, I took it and joined her inside.

I was officially sitting in the back of a police car on December twenty-third. If that's not Christmas card worthy, I don't know what is.

CHAPTER 3

"Have you ever ridden in the back of one of these?" Brittany asked.

Strange. Her voice held a note of pain. That's when I realized I'd been squeezing her hand. "Sorry," I said, letting go.

Britt took my hand back. "I wasn't complaining."

I sighed. "You should have told me."

Brittany's voice was almost intimate as she said, "I think you're avoiding the question."

Was Britt trying to flirt? What question was she even talking about? Oh, right.

She was trying to distract me, since riding in the back of a cop car left me crushing her hand. Let's see...Her question was something like *Had I ever been caged in the back of a cop car?* If I played along, maybe it would help Britt feel productive.

"Have I ever ridden in the back of a cop car?" I repeated. When she nodded, I lowered my voice to whisper in her ear, "I'll tell if you tell."

"Holt!" Brittany shoved my arm while surprised laughter burbled out.

Just then the car hit a patch of ice, and I swallowed a yell. It was over in a moment. The officer easily regained traction, but it was way too soon considering our near miss. Why hadn't Mom chosen Christmas in the desert?

"Holt?"

"Hm?"

"You can let go now. We're fine," Britt said.

Had I been squishing her hand again? But no. That wasn't the problem. I'd reached my arm across Brittany and was pinning her to the back of the seat.

"Oh," I said, removing my arm. "Sorry. I don't remember doing that."

Brittany rested her head on my shoulder. "That was really impressive."

The strange thing was she was serious. And how could Britt be so relaxed given everything that had happened?

I sat back a bit, but my whole body was rigid. Britt was so great, *I love you* almost slipped from my mouth. I stopped myself just in time. I said the only thing I could get away with in the back of a cop car. "You're pretty great."

"Right back at ya," she said.

I winced in the darkness. This wasn't chickening out. If I ever told Britt *I love you*, it would be spontaneous and romantic—not from the back of a police cruiser after finding a dead body.

The problem was, I was running out of ways to *not* say it. This wasn't the first time I'd almost said it by accident. We'd been dating for around six months. Now should be a perfectly reasonable time to let her know how I felt. I maybe would have if it weren't for Thanksgiving.

The vehicle slowed, and the turn signal began clicking. We'd arrived at the gas station while I'd been stuck overthinking my relationship. Though was I really overthinking? Saying *I love you* was a big deal. I'd only said it to my college girlfriend, and Tasha had definitely said it first.

I doubt I even loved Tasha at the time. More it was just the expected thing to say…It's a wonder Tasha hadn't dumped me sooner.

Cop #2 had to open my door to let me out. If I pretended I was in the back of a limo and he was my chauffeur, it made the experience less dreadful than the reality of temporary incarceration.

The station's parking lot was super icy, and I almost fell twice on the short walk to the mini-mart. Brittany was fine. Then again, Brittany was wearing snow boots while I was in shoes.

Inside the mini-mart were the usual aisles of junk food, and along the back wall there were a few sets of little round bistro tables with pairs of chairs set up. We were directed to sit down while the two cops murmured to each other just out of earshot.

"Don't you have to *go*?" Britt asked, tilting her head toward the restrooms just past the checkout counter.

"Well," I said, "they told us to stay here." It was probably irrational, but I didn't want to be yelled at for leaving my spot at the table.

"Uh-huh." Brittany's eyes sparkled—somehow she found my discomfort amusing.

"Here," Cop #1 said, returning to our table with a couple of Styrofoam cups. "Some hot cocoa should warm you up."

Brittany and I shared a look. This wasn't the first murder investigation we'd been a part of with a hot cocoa enthusiast. At least now it was Christmastime, which made hot cocoa seasonally appropriate. Plus, I was freezing.

Britt's lips trembled, and when I took a long drink, she winked. Hopefully it was some form of shock, but I was very close to bursting out laughing and all because an officer had brought us some hot chocolate.

I had to leave before the temptation to laugh overtook me. "Excuse me," I said, standing and nodding in the direction of the restrooms.

"Of course," the officer said. "I'll start getting information from Ms. Asato."

I sighed as I made my way across the store. I couldn't ignore the inevitable anymore—I'd have to use a gas station bathroom.

As it turned out, both of the single-occupancy bathrooms were being used. Which meant I had to wait a little longer. Too bad since I was growing increasingly uncomfortable.

While I stood waiting, shifting slowly from side to side trying to avoid looking like a grown man about to pee his pants, footage appeared on the screen by the checkout counter. Cop #2 was watching with the gas station attendant. The camera they were looking at gave a view of the side road.

The clerk was explaining how the recordings were motion sensitive and only saved footage when there was movement. I took out my phone and, pretending to text, slowly shuffled farther from the bathrooms to get a better view of the screen.

The cop was taking notes as the recording played. "Okay, here's where our victim's car drove by. Then came a silver sedan and about five minutes later a black truck."

A middle-aged woman exited the bathroom, but I lingered by the register.

"This looks like Holt Jacobs's vehicle. He was the one who called it in." Afterward the camera showed nothing but the string of flashing emergency vehicles.

A trucker left the second bathroom. I was really running low on time.

"Can we check other cameras to get license plate numbers?" Cop #2 asked the clerk.

"Bathroom's open," a voice said behind me.

I jumped. Cop #1, who'd been with Britt, stood looking down at me and my attempts at amateur sleuthing.

Caught with my hand in a metaphorical cookie jar, I decided the best route was distraction. "Right, thanks," I said, frowning down at my phone. "Sorry. I was attaching this video from the crime scene to an email and the Wi-Fi's super slow."

It was a mostly true statement.

Cop #1 looked from me to Cop #2 by the monitor, still skeptical about my real motives for loitering by the cash register.

Time to lay it on thicker. "Do you have an email I should send it to?"

He handed me a business card with a police email listed, and in a few keystrokes I'd sent them my video.

"There you go." I gave my best laid-back smile. "Now, if you'll excuse me," and I went into the closest restroom.

Once in the bathroom, I couldn't help rolling my eyes at my reflection.

What was I doing?

Without detailing the experience, I will say the gas station bathroom was in much better shape than expected. There wasn't any graffiti or carvings on the walls. Plus, the floor wasn't sticky.

I wasn't excited to face the police again. They thought I was an armchair detective—or worse, a garden-variety busybody. However, (and this is embarrassing to admit), I was looking forward to drinking more hot chocolate since my feet were still numb.

Britt and Cop #1 were talking through her statement when I sat back down and took a few gulps of the sugary hot chocolate.

"Ms. Asato filled out your basic information," the officer said. "Can you look it over and verify it's correct?"

A quick glance showed everything was in order. I frowned. How did Brittany know all the details? I didn't even know her address. I knew how to get to her apartment, but I wouldn't be able to write it down on a form.

I nodded at the officer. "It's all good."

Brittany's hand found my knee under the table. "I hope I didn't overstep."

I shrugged. This really wasn't a conversation I wanted to have while sharing a bistro table with a police officer.

Shrugging wasn't good enough for Brittany. She gave my knee a squeeze. "I've had so many emergency calls where friends and family can't fill out the most basic info." Brittany moved to tuck an invisible strand of hair behind her ear. "I make sure to know all those details for people I'm close to."

"Makes sense." There didn't need to be anything creepy about memorizing my personal info. I managed a grin. "The problem is you're making me look bad. I'd be writing *Britt* instead of *Brittany* and guessing a middle initial."

"You'd do just fine." There was an intensity in Brittany's eyes that I couldn't quite place.

Heat rose up my neck—probably from the hot chocolate. My voice was husky when I said, "Definitely."

Cop #1 asked, "Mr. Jacobs, can you explain the video you sent?"

I guess the officer's cockles weren't warmed by the sincere display of affection playing out in front of him.

Isn't Christmas the season to amp up the PDA? All I can say is, *A bah-humbug to you, sir.*

The officer asked me a few more questions and had us sign our statements. By the end, the guy knew more about me than most of my coworkers. He had my home address, my vacation address, and a front-row seat to just how crazy I was about Brittany.

His partner was still reviewing footage with the gas station attendant when our officer finished up with us. Our cop excused himself and joined the other two.

Yawning, I leaned back in my chair and stretched out my legs. I don't know if it's a shock thing, but I get unreasonably tired after finding a dead body.

Brittany gave my leg another squeeze. "We're almost done."

Moving my chair so it was right next to hers, I wrapped my arm around her. "I don't know how you do your job every day. One dead body and I'm wiped."

Britt rested her head against me. "I actually like that dead bodies bother you."

I stiffened. What was that supposed to mean?

"You care," Brittany added.

The way she said it, I sounded like a good person. A grin played at my lips. Suddenly our seats in a fluorescent-lit gas station mini-mart felt intimate and cozy. Should I tell her I loved her even if she didn't say it back?

"We'll bring you back to your car now," our cop said, shattering my moment of warmth and goodwill.

I finished the dregs of my hot chocolate, then followed Britt and the two officers back to the patrol car, where I voluntarily got into the back of a police cruiser for the second time in one night.

While I don't know the exact depth, it seemed an additional inch or two of snow had coated the road during our time at the gas station. I really wasn't looking forward to the final drive to get to Mom's Christmas lodge.

The problem with a *white Christmas* is it's extremely dangerous to drive in.

Emergency vehicles were still at the crash site, with the flashing red and blue lights illuminating the roadway.

The officers parked and escorted Britt and me to our car. After cranking on the heat, I left Brittany in the warmth of the rental to knock snow off the windows. The two officers hadn't returned to the crime scene but instead were shining their flashlights farther down the road. They were talking to each other and pointing at something in the snow.

Then I saw them. Almost buried by the fresh snow and the drifting were faint indents of footprints.

Had someone left the crime scene on foot?

"Can we help you?" the first officer asked. He wouldn't be impressed with the theories of an armchair detective, so I shook my head and got back in the car.

At first when I tried to leave my impromptu parking spot, the car barely budged and the tires squealed in the snow. I really didn't want to ask the police officers for a push...or if I could borrow a shovel. I held my breath and rocked the vehicle back and forth before giving a spontaneous cheer when the car moved onto the road. I sobered up immediately when the tires skidded, but we quickly regained control.

This was like an adult version of "Little Red Riding Hood," only instead of a big bad wolf along the way, there were ax murderers. What would happen when I reached Grandmother's house? If any of my family suddenly had enormously large teeth, we'd be leaving.

I drove slowly in the snow, but it felt like I had control of the vehicle. If anything, the fresh snow was covering the icy sections, giving the tires something to grip. I mean, I was still white-knuckling the steering wheel, but that could have been for any number of reasons.

Thankfully, Brittany stayed quiet. She watched the road as intently as I did, though occasionally she turned her head in my direction.

Could she tell my nerves were shot? So close to arriving at my mother's marvelous Christmas and I was too wound up about ice axes and icy roads to worry about my family hanging out with Britt.

Our turn for the house was coming up, and the GPS had the road dead-ending up ahead. Momentarily, I considered driving to the end of the road to check for vehicles from the footage. But that would take explaining my snooping to Brittany, and we'd both dealt with enough stressors for one night. Besides, there was a decent chance Mom was watching from the house and she'd comment on my choice to drive past our lodgings.

My turn signal was on and I was slowing down when an ATV with a snowplow attached appeared at the end of the driveway.

Please realize I'm not happy about this, but the ATV's driver looked like Santa Claus. He wore the traditional red hat with white fur and had a long white beard. The fake Santa also wore red suspenders and a light plaid flannel coat that he hadn't bothered to button.

Now, I'm just going to say this once. The guy with the white bushy beard and red suspenders wasn't Santa. This isn't one of those stories where you go, *Did Holt meet the real Santa?*

He wasn't the real Santa, just an eccentric old man who liked to dress up. I know this because, according to tradition, Santa lives in the North Pole. Mr. Claus wouldn't spend December twenty-third in the middle of Montana plowing my mom's driveway when the busiest night of his year was only a few hours away.

Still, it was weird.

"You see him?" Britt asked.

"Yup," I said.

The fake Santa waved as he turned and drove up the road that was dead-ending. If I had to guess, he was heading to the house that had a sleigh with nine reindeer lit up on the roof.

After watching him a little longer than strictly necessary, I turned at the private drive. A little ways up stood a large cabin with Christmas lights glittering against the snow.

I don't know how often the ATV Santa plowed, but what if we got trapped in there? I shuddered. As much as I disliked Mom's need to have tons of scheduled outings, being stuck in one house with my entire family for days...Well, let's just say it would be inhumane and could lead to a gripping true crime story—murder sells around the holidays.

"Do you think we'll get snowed in?" I asked.

"Absolutely not," Britt said, so authoritatively that I got the impression she was overcompensating.

While the driveway was long enough to get trapped in, it also ended way too soon and left me with no other option than to park next to the row of vehicles near the large cabin.

Brittany let out a breath. "We made it."

I nodded. While the winter driving had been successfully completed, this felt like one of those situations that is best described as *out of the frying pan and into the fire*.

"...Holt?" Britt's hand was on my shoulder.

"Yeah?"

"Are you ready to head in? I think we're being watched."

Oh, we were definitely being watched. The only question was *how many* people were watching.

"Uh-huh," I said.

I unbuckled and got out of the car, then grabbed my luggage. Britt had likewise gathered her belongings, and I took the final bag, which held gifts for all my relatives—yet another reason I prefer gift cards.

There was a freshly shoveled path leading to the covered wraparound porch. Squaring my shoulders, I said, "Let's go," before leading the way into the lion's den.

CHAPTER 4

Dad was waiting at the wide-open door. He gave me a big bear hug while my arms were still full of suitcases. We'd seen each other in May, yet with my parents moving to a different continent, this reunion held more weight.

When Dad let go, I was able to get into the entryway, where I was greeted with the scent of Christmas baking and Michael Bublé singing "Santa Claus Is Coming to Town." The music made sense. I can't remember a Christmas season when Mom didn't have Michael Bublé's Christmas album playing in the background.

It really was Christmas.

"...meet you. I'm Brittany," she was saying as she shook hands with Dad.

Yikes. How had I messed up already? It was my job to make introductions.

"Nice to meet you," Dad said. "Come on in. Gladys and Casey are baking in the kitchen."

We set down our bags, removed our shoes, and followed Dad through our home for the next few days.

The place was a massive three-story log cabin, with huge exposed beams stretching across the ceiling, which somehow still managed to be rustic even with its size. Christmas decor was everywhere, from lights to garlands and various sizes of Christmas trees. A gas fireplace was burning in the living room, with a decorative mantel ready for Mom to hang all our stockings.

"Did you pay extra for the deluxe Christmas package?" I asked as we passed a banister where each post was wrapped in red ribbon like they were candy canes.

Brittany let out a surprised laugh, while all Dad did was give a slight shake of his head with the cryptic reply of "You know your mother."

Entering the kitchen, we were greeted with an open oven and my sister Casey removing a pan of gingerbread men as Mom quickly filled the oven with a new pan of unbaked cookies.

It was an idyllic holiday scene...and then Mom started talking.

"About time you showed up," she said, putting her hands on her hips and giving me the *mom once-over.* "You were scheduled to make cookies this evening. Casey had to fill in for you."

Merry Christmas, everyone.

Then Mom smiled. "Would you relax? I'm kidding."

I frowned, but before I could say something snarky, Mom had wrapped her arms around me.

"Mom..." I said, struggling to break free when she didn't let go.

"Oh, am I embarrassing you in front of your girlfriend?" Mom asked loud enough for everyone to hear.

I winced and suddenly realized I had a headache.

"Hello, Mrs. Jacobs. It's good to see you again." Britt was smiling, but it didn't reach her eyes.

"Call me Gladys," Mom said, and Britt nodded.

A pang of bitterness hit. The only name I was given for Britt's mom was Mrs. Asato. Come to think of it, I didn't even know her first name.

Casey greeted me with "You look tired." Though, to be fair, I'd kind of tuned out the room for a few seconds, so she probably had a point. My sister handed me a fresh cookie and gave me a quick hug.

"Tomorrow's an early start," she said. "You both might want to get to bed."

I looked at Brittany, and she nodded. "Sounds good," I said.

"All right." Mom was all business. "Brittany, your room's on the top floor across from Jude and Juniper. Holt, you'll be sleeping through there."

I raised an eyebrow. The door Mom was pointing to looked like it went to a broom closet. Walking over, I opened the door, and instead of a broom closet, I found a pantry with a twin-size air mattress dominating the space.

"Mom?" I asked, since I really had no other words for spending my Christmas on an air mattress in a closet.

Mom had moved on from room assignments to rolling out more cookie dough. I smoothed back my hair, accepting the hand I was dealt. Another real bedroom, with a real mattress, wasn't going to magically appear. I was stuck in the pantry.

"Uh..." I turned to Brittany. "Let me help you with your bags."

Britt took her carry-on, while I grabbed the suitcase and the bag with all the gifts—there was no way I was cramming the extra bag into the pantry. Casey walked us upstairs. "Here's the second-floor bathroom," she said, pointing. "Brittany, you might want to use this one tonight since Juniper's showering upstairs. I'm with Nigel and the kids in these two rooms, while Mom and Dad are through there."

"Thanks, sis," I said, hoping she'd take the hint and let me have a private goodbye with Brittany on the third floor. From Casey's smirk, you'd think I was a teenager trying to sneak my girlfriend behind the garage for my first kiss, instead of her older (and wiser) brother.

"Brittany, your room will be the door to the left." Then, imitating one of Mom's all-knowing faces, Casey winked at me before telling Britt it was nice to officially meet and going to her room.

We headed up the final flight of stairs to get to Britt's room. For a bedroom, it was small. Nothing but a twin bed under the eaves and a small antique dresser, but compared to the storage closet I'd be bunking in, it was five-star accommodations.

I sighed as I looked at Britt's real bed with a real mattress.

"Do you want to trade?" Britt asked. Her lips twitched, and I had the annoying suspicion she was trying not to laugh.

"Are you kidding?" I sat on the foot of the bed, feeling the mattress's natural give beneath me—something air mattresses don't replicate. "Mom would kill me if I made my girlfriend sleep on an air mattress while I got a bed."

"Oh," Britt said, her eyes beginning to sparkle. "But if your mom weren't here, I'd be banished to the pantry?"

I grinned. "Absolutely. And I wouldn't bother with the air mattress. Sleep on the floor, Cinderella, and make friends with the mice."

Brittany came to stand in front of me. "Has anyone ever accused you of being a Scrooge?"

"Maybe once or twice." And I winked when she giggled.

Standing up, I gave Brittany an appropriately long good night kiss before actually saying good night.

Casey was waiting for me on the second floor. "So?" she asked.

"So?"

"How is it?"

I raised my eyebrows, and Casey rolled her eyes.

"How are things with you and Brittany?"

"Good."

"Come on. Give me more. I've never met one of your girlfriends before."

"Fine," I said. "Umm...I like her."

"Well, that's"—Casey tapped a finger to her chin—"vague."

The problem with Casey is since she became a mom, she's grown more and more like our mom. The wheels were turning as she tried to figure out the best way to get the information she wanted. It took her a few seconds to land on the right thing to say.

"Mom said you were in Seattle for Thanksgiving, while Brittany spent it with her family in Oregon."

Wow. That, folks, is called a *loaded statement*. Here's the thing, it was a *statement*, and the trick is not to answer implied questions. All I said was "Yeah, my buddy Darren and I ate at my place and watched football."

Before Casey could rephrase to ask why I hadn't joined Britt's family, I added, "I need to get to bed. Good night, sis." Then I beat a hasty retreat to the ground floor.

I got my bag and walked past Dad in the living room. He was settled into a recliner, reading from a very thick book. I paused at the ground-floor bathroom and washed up on my way to the pantry. Then I was in the kitchen about to enter my assigned room. For Britt's sake, I should behave and not whine about my banishment to a place that smelled like a storage room.

"Wait a minute," Mom called.

My shoulders fell. She'd caught me. I turned around to find her waiting expectantly.

Mom shook her head. "Relax. I only have ninety seconds before the timer beeps. You can leave when it goes off. Understood?"

I nodded.

"Now, do the police have theories on your murderer?"

I shrugged. A trail of boot prints leading away from the crime scene wasn't an actual suspect.

"Did they tell you anything?"

I frowned. "They were asking me the questions. They weren't sharing their suspect list."

Mom's timer beeped just as she opened her mouth to ask another question I wouldn't be able to answer.

"Good night," I said and disappeared into the pantry.

With my suitcase in the small space, there were maybe two square feet of space to maneuver in, and I banged my elbow twice on a bag of rice while trying to change into a pair of joggers.

Besides the room being small, it amplified any kitchen clatter and was colder than the rest of the house. A long-sleeve shirt wasn't warm enough, so I added a pullover and considered putting on a hat.

I grumbled to myself as I got under the covers. This was going to be one long vacation.

The one plus side to my tiny quarters was I could turn the light off from bed. Right as I flicked off the switch, there was a knock at the door. "Come in," I said, hoping it would be Brittany but expecting Mom with more questions about the murder.

I was wrong.

The woman who appeared in the doorway was my one and only baby sister, Juniper—oh, and Chouzie, her reddish chow chow that made a living on social media. She turned on the light and came to sit on the edge of the air mattress, wobbling slightly as it shifted. "Good, you're up," she said.

When my only reply was a glare, she asked, "What, no hello?"

I was too tired for this. Giving my fakest smile, I said, "Hello, Juniper. What a surprise."

She ignored the attitude, too busy examining the food options on the pantry shelves. "You're lucky to sleep here."

I raised an eyebrow. "Lucky?"

"Uh-huh. If you wake up in the middle of the night with a craving, you won't even need to get out of bed."

"I guess," I said. Then I rested my head against my pillow as a yawn overtook me.

That earned me a smack on the arm. "Holt, you can't fall asleep yet."

Rolling to my side so my back was to her, I closed my eyes and said, "Give me a break. I'm an old man, and it's past my bedtime."

"You're thirty," Juniper said. When that didn't work, she began shaking me, making the whole air mattress move. "Come on. Mom and Dad are still awake."

My only answer was a fake snore.

Juniper huffed out a breath. "I can't believe this. No one tells me anything anymore. Mom won't say why you were delayed, but I heard her say something to Dad about *Holt finding another dead body*. Then, when I see Brittany, all she says is..."

So, I actually fell asleep during Juniper's impassioned speech. Not only was I wiped from the day, but hearing Juniper complain about the one time things didn't go her way wasn't exactly riveting.

I woke up when Juniper pinched my earlobe. "Stop it," I grumbled. "Or I'll tell Mom."

Juniper pointed a finger in my face. "Tattletale. Just tell me what I want to know, and we can all be happy."

Had Juniper taken a course on effective torture tactics for the twenty-first century? I suspected her husband, Jude, was some sort of spy. Could he have taken her to that seminar?

"Please, Holt?" Juniper had transformed her face to innocent baby sister. Then Chouzie gave a low bark in agreement. I was outnumbered.

Knowing I'd probably regret it but being too tired to care, I picked up my phone and set up the video I'd taken of the crime scene. Maybe I should have warned Juniper about the man with the ice ax, but it's not like I'd been warned when I found him in person.

Her eyes bugged out at the sight. "How did that happen?" She froze the image and shoved the phone in my face. She'd turned the screen's brightness way up, and I squinted at the light.

"That's what the police are looking into," I said. "Now go."

"But Mom said a car accident. Wasn't there a car accident?"

"I don't know. Probably."

"But he didn't die in the crash?" Juniper asked.

That earned her a glare. You didn't have to be a coroner to know the man hadn't died in the crash.

But Juniper wasn't done asking questions. "Do you think the car crash was from the ice or someone forced it to happen?"

I raised my head to look at her. "How would they have forced it to happen?"

"I don't know." Juniper tossed her hair. "Spike strips across the road?"

"Spike strips? Are you serious? This isn't *Need for Speed: Montana*."

Juniper stuck her tongue out. "Well, I'm not seeing you come up with any helpful suggestions."

"Seeing as Brittany and I almost slid off the road at that same spot, I think the crash was accidental."

"Maybe the killer poured something on the road to make it extra slick."

"Sure," I said.

"You think?" Juniper made the whole air mattress bounce in her excitement.

"No. I don't think the killer poured black ice across the road. Now go away. I'm sleeping."

"How can you sleep with an actual ax murderer in the woods?" Instead of trembling with fear, Juniper's voice was high with excitement.

Pulling the comforter above my shoulders, I said, "Easy. There's no way he'd look in the pantry."

CHAPTER 5

I vaguely remember Juniper turning off the lights and leaving...Chouzie may have licked my hand. Sometime later rustling sounds woke me up with a jolt. When I sat up and forced my eyes open, at first all I could make out was someone in the pantry rifling through the shelves.

An unintelligible sound came from my mouth. Something that was meant to strike fear in the heart of any ax murderer.

"Sorry, champ." Dad's voice. Dad had broken in. I was safe. "I just need the coffee. Go back to sleep."

"Is it morning?" I asked, reaching to check my phone before Dad answered.

"It's early," he said. "No one else is up."

He left with the coffee, and I flopped back against the bed.

While I'd joked with Juniper about ax murderers, I was a little jumpy. My heart was pounding after waking up to sounds in my room. There was no way I could fall back to sleep, so I got up and headed for the shower.

I took my time washing up and doing my hair. Time spent alone on family vacations is rare, and it's important to savor the moments when you can.

Last night I'd been distracted. Still, I couldn't remember seeing any other homes or driveways on the way to our Christmas cabin. Also, if the road dead-ended nearby, the two cars of murder suspects on the video must live close to our house.

I was quickly distracted from the car conundrum by a more urgent question. Should I shave? Usually during vacations I'll grow some version of sexy scruff. That look would work well in Montana. The problem was, Christmas was a time when lots of photos were taken, and I didn't want to look bedraggled in the photos Mom posted without my permission.

In the end I decided to be clean shaven this holiday season. I'd just started shaving when an infernal racket began outside the bathroom. The razor slipped, and I nicked my chin.

I couldn't tell what was happening with the bathroom fan on. Opening the door, I peeked my head out. There were Casey and Nigel's two kids, dressed in pajamas and dancing around the living room singing something unrecognizable. The tune may have been a Christmas song, but I couldn't say for sure.

Easing the door shut, I took a deep breath. Everything would be fine. Sure, I already had a headache and the day hadn't really started yet. But that was fine. Headaches were normal for family vacations.

With the racket Harper and Baxter were making, it was easy to exit the bathroom without being spotted. I'm usually the master of slipping around places unnoticed. What tripped me up was having my *bedroom* right off the kitchen. I'd made it safely through the dining room without any conversations. Both of my brothers-in-law were in there, but they're the good sort who mind their own business.

There was even a chance I could have made it from the kitchen to the pantry, but I gave myself up when I saw Mom showing Britt photos on her phone.

Couldn't Mom wait till I'd had coffee before she started embarrassing me?

"This is us last Christmas morning in California," Mom was saying as I joined the two of them.

The photo showed the rest of my family sitting prominently on a couch and the floor, all wearing matching blue pajamas with snowflakes on them. I was nothing more than a floating head in the image since Mom made me kneel behind the couch.

"And here's the year before," Mom said, showing a similar photo. This time Harper was a tiny baby, and the matching pajamas were Christmas-light themed—I was still a floating head in the background.

Britt raised an eyebrow. "I'm sensing a pattern."

I ran a hand through my hair. "The Mother's Day tradition is matching T-shirts, and for Christmas, it's matching pajamas."

"A tradition *someone* refuses to participate in." Mom's tone held parental disapproval, like me declining to put on a pale blue onesie was a character flaw.

"Forcing me to kneel behind a couch for five minutes to hide my body keeps your perfect aesthetic."

I expected Mom to continue our argument. Instead, she turned to Brittany and asked, "Will you wear the matching pajamas Christmas morning?"

"Uh..." Britt shot me a confused look.

"I guessed your size and bought you a pair in case you're more fun than Holt."

I was opening my mouth to object, when Britt said, "Of course."

"Wonderful," Mom said, knowing how to take the win. Then she added, "Maybe you can talk Ebenezer Scrooge into joining."

I had to lock my jaw to keep myself from saying something rude, and Mom knew me well enough to leave the kitchen immediately.

"You know you don't have to wear the matching pajamas?" I asked.

"Come on." Brittany gave me a playful shove. "It'll be fun."

"What would make you agree to this?"

Tucking invisible strands of hair behind her ears, Britt asked, "Is it so bad to have your Mom like me?"

I sighed. "The humiliation of matching pajamas can't be worth the gold stars Mom will hand out."

Britt shook her head, but she didn't seem frustrated. "You really are a Scrooge."

For some reason, I grinned at that. "Well, I haven't had my coffee yet."

Brittany gasped like I'd just confessed to a secret hatred of sunglasses. While tempted to keep teasing her, I prioritized pouring myself the inaugural first cup of coffee.

"You know," Britt said after I had a few sips, "your mother gave me the very important mission of convincing you to wear the pj's."

I choked on the coffee.

Once I'd stopped choking, I said, "Not happening. Ever."

"Why not?"

"For starters, it's tacky. Also"—I leaned in close—"I'm her son. She's genetically programmed to like me." I gave Britt's nose a quick tap and grinned when her lips quirked as she fought her own smile.

"Say," I said, remembering the cars in the security footage, "did Mom mention when the family fun is beginning?"

"It's on the schedule."

I groaned. "Not you, too. I need a partner on this trip, not another person telling me I'm running late for sand museums or bear tours."

Brittany raised an eyebrow. "Bear tours?"

I shuddered. That little gem had happened three years ago. "Don't ask."

"Fine." Britt poured more coffee into my mug—was the refill a hint I was being cranky, or was my girlfriend being thoughtful? "To answer the original question, we're scheduled to be at the vehicles in fifty minutes."

"Great." I set my mug on the counter. "Then there's time for a walk."

"A walk?" The scar by Britt's eyebrow grew more defined.

My jaw ticked. Britt's concern about me walking was a little offensive. I work out regularly and am in great shape. Granted, I choose a gym over communing with nature, but she didn't need to be so surprised.

"I saw some footage at the gas station, and I wanted to check out the neighboring cars." Brittany was watching me with one of her unreadable expressions. "Do you want to come?" I tried.

"Sure," Britt said, but I still didn't know what she was thinking. Then, we agreed to meet at the front door after we were dressed for the winter weather.

When I got to the entryway, Brittany was waiting, and she wasn't alone. I swallowed a groan and was glad I'd already put on my sunglasses.

Casey was helping Harper into boots and Baxter was fully outfitted, and Juniper...Juniper was watching the whole thing like she expected a show.

When Brittany saw me, her eyes lit up. "I hope it's all right if Baxter and Harper come, too. They've been wanting to go outside since they woke up. I told Casey we could watch them."

Nodding slowly, I managed to say, "Great."

Of course. Why not bring children on a murder investigation?

Baxter was chanting, "Snow, snow, snow," by the door while jumping up and down. Was I ever that energetic?

Casey put a hat on Harper before saying she was ready to go. Harper did her best to walk to where Baxter was waiting, but she was so small, and Casey had her so bundled up in a puffy coat, snow pants, boots, hat, and mittens that Harper wasn't getting anywhere fast. In all her layers, she kind of resembled a bright pink roly-poly.

As Harper made it past me, she paused for a moment to look shyly up at me. "My hat's pink," she said.

Not sure how to reply, I said, "That's a good color." Harper seemed satisfied and moved on without further comment.

I frowned as she shuffled away. Juniper came to stand beside me. "Something on your mind?"

Leaning close, I whispered, "Since when did Harper start talking?"

"Oh, Holt." Juniper widened her eyes like I'd just said something adorable and walked away.

I wasn't kidding. Sure it was December, but when I last saw Harper in May, her vocabulary was limited to a few names. Was it normal to be speaking in sentences seven months later?

"Everyone ready?" Britt asked, opening the door.

Harper and Baxter both cheered before grabbing Britt's hands and dragging her out of the house.

The kids had only met Brittany this morning and they were already good friends. How was that possible? Was Brittany magic?

We were still on the porch when we all froze. A police car had parked beside my rental, and the two cops from last night were getting out. Suddenly Harper and Baxter were hiding behind Brittany's legs—like they really thought the cops couldn't see them.

"Morning," I said. And somehow I was standing in front of Brittany, like that would make her invisible.

"Morning," Cop #1 said as they walked to the front porch.

"Did you need something?" I asked, trying to think of a good reason for them to be here.

The second cop shook his head. "You and Ms. Asato already gave your statements, and those two"—he gestured to where Baxter was peeking his head out—"are too young, but we're conducting interviews with people who live along this road in case anyone saw something."

"Okay." I glanced from them to the door. What was I expected to do? Would Mom be mad if I just continued with my walk like I hadn't seen the officers?

Before I'd reached a decision, the front door opened and Dad stood there. "What's going on?" he asked. The question sounded so calm, so natural, you'd think he was used to police showing up to his home.

"We're following up about last night's car crash," Cop #1 said. "We're making sure no one here saw anything."

"The *crash*?" Dad asked me, not the officers.

"Yes." Cop #2 looked at me pointedly. "The crash."

I nodded. Did the police really expect me not to tell anyone about the ice ax? And it's not like I'd told my whole family what happened. Only my parents...and Juniper...who'd probably told Jude. But Casey's family, none of them should know about the ax murderer.

"Do you need them?" Dad asked, nodding toward me and the three people clustered behind me.

"No, sir, we don't," said Cop #2.

"Good," Dad said. "Go ahead with your walk. I'm sure we'll be fine."

"Sure thing," I said. But I didn't move as Dad stepped inside and the police followed him in.

After the door clicked shut, Britt nudged me. "We should go. I'm sure it's just interviews. The kids could use a distraction."

She was right. Of course she was right. Still, it took a conscious effort to turn away from the house and begin walking.

The driveway had been plowed again, but I was stuck meandering beside Brittany and the kids. Harper made steady progress but slow enough that Baxter let go of Brittany's hand and began running and leaping about. *Easy* for an adult to walk through in snow boots and *easy* for a little kid bundled like a roly-poly to walk through are two *very* different things.

Britt was just telling Baxter to be careful when he stumbled and was half-buried in a snow berm. Baxter began to cry even as Britt employed her calm paramedic voice. "Stay still. I'll get you out."

Before I had a chance to react, Brittany had scooped up Harper and set her in my arms.

Nope.

Children don't like me.

Did Britt want both kids crying?

Chapter 6

For a second neither Harper nor I knew what to do. Then Harper's eyes watered, and her bottom lip began trembling.

"Please don't," I said—not that I expected to reason with a miniature human.

Hearing my voice, Harper scrunched up her face in confusion. She reached a mittened hand to my face and tapped at my sunglasses.

Oh no.

"You want me to take off my sunglasses?"

Harper's watery eyes stared solemnly up at me.

Not wanting her to start crying, I chose the unthinkable. "Okay, kid," I said and removed my sunglasses. The sun bouncing off the white snow was positively blinding. Squinting, I frowned down at Harper. "Is this what you wanted?"

She giggled.

Go figure.

My eyes were half-closed to block the glare as I continued down the driveway with Harper.

Baxter had been all right the moment Britt had removed him from the snow berm, and the two of them were running to the bottom of the long driveway.

Harper bounced a little in my arms and said, "Race!"

This kid already had me remove my sunglasses in a sun-glare vortex. Did she really expect me to start running downhill through snow and ice while carrying my only niece? The way Harper kept bouncing in my arms, it was clear that was exactly what she wanted.

What had Brittany gotten me into?

I wasn't willing to go fast enough to outrun the other two, but I did begin jogging. There was strange shaking in my arms as Harper began laughing.

Huh. This wasn't too bad.

Then I stumbled against a chunk of ice I hadn't noticed since I was jogging with my eyes half-closed.

Instead of worrying about self-preservation, I instinctively held Harper tighter. While I was able to regain my footing, it still rattled me, and I continued the rest of the way down at a slower speed.

Do I have paternal instincts?

The other two were waiting for us by the road. Once we made it down, Harper wiggled out of my arms. She attempted to run only to trip with all her clothing and face-plant against the snow-packed road.

Harper began wailing. This is why you don't bring miniature humans on murder investigations. I shot Britt a dirty look—granted Brittany didn't actually see it since she was too busy comforting Harper.

We'd watched Casey's children for less than ten minutes, and in that time they'd both begun weeping. Is this why people want kids?

Oh, and Harper was fine. With how Casey had her bundled up, Harper could have fallen off the roof without any injuries.

Britt had picked Harper up, but as soon as Harper saw me, she held her arms out to me.

What?

There I was holding my crying niece when I was supposed to be conducting a private murder investigation. If she cried for too long, Britt would make us go back. And if Mom spotted us, we'd be unable to resume the investigation, since she'd say it was time for whatever event she'd scheduled.

My only option was to get Harper to calm down. I decided on a tactic that usually worked with Juniper.

Distraction.

"Do you see that brick house?"

Nothing. Harper clung to me and continued sobbing.

At least those homeowners had gotten into the Christmas spirit, so I tried again. "Do you see the reindeer on the roof?"

That caught Harper's attention. She stopped mid-sob, and her head shot up to find the reindeer.

"They're pretty cool," I said and was rewarded with a giggle.

Then she pointed to the roof. "Santa!"

Santa?

It wasn't hard to spot who Harper was pointing at. I expected to find a fake Santa to go with the reindeer. But this Mr. Claus was crouched strangely on the roof between the sleigh and the first reindeer.

Then he moved—not in a mechanical way. My grip on Harper momentarily loosened. That was a human being. It was the old man who'd plowed our driveway last night.

"Santa!" Harper cried again.

The stranger on the roof heard and stood up. "Ho, ho, ho"—the guy really committed—"have you been a good girl this year?"

Harper nodded emphatically, suddenly too shy to talk.

"Good for you. I'll see you tonight."

Creepy. So creepy. I know I'm supposed to go, *Aww isn't that sweet*, but a strange man just told my niece he would see her tonight. I don't care if he is the real Santa. I was cutting off all contact, and I hurried the two of us past his house.

At this point Harper was content being a silent passenger, and I was able to investigate in peace.

To say Mom's cabin was part of a massive mountain cul-de-sac is a bit of an exaggeration, but it isn't that far off. There were four other driveways along the road as it looped around to double back on itself.

The brick house with the reindeer had no visible vehicles. Sure, either the silver sedan or the black truck could belong there and they were parked in the garage next to the ATV. But creepy or not, even I didn't want a Santa impersonator to be a murderer over the holidays.

The next house we walked past was closer to the road and had two white passenger vans parked out front.

A group of teens were yelling amateurish threats as they hurled snowballs. I shuddered. Even at thirty I had yet to recover from all the *fun* youth trips Mom had *encouraged* me to attend. They were always extremely loud, and there was never enough sleep.

"They're having fun," Britt said.

I did a double take to make sure Brittany was serious. "Right," I said.

There must've been sarcasm in my tone, because Britt's eyes sparkled. "Sorry, Grandpa, I forgot. No fun's allowed."

As a nickname, *Grandpa* is not my favorite.

"I like fun," I said. Then added to be more playful, "Just as long as it doesn't get too loud or interfere with my bedtime."

"Or your nap time," Britt said.

Before I could answer, Harper said, "I have a nap time."

A warm chuckle came from somewhere deep inside of me. Where had that come from? Clearing my throat, I told Harper, "I really like taking naps."

"I don't," Harper said, before getting distracted and bouncing a little in my arms when a nearby teen was hit full in the face by a snowball.

"Careful, Holt," Brittany said. "If Juniper saw you with that smile, she'd accuse you of being a soft, warm teddy bear on the inside."

Even though I should have been annoyed, for a moment with Brittany backlit by the snow, I almost said *I love you*. Like, the words almost slipped out.

What was with me? I needed to keep that sentence buried deep inside.

I guess my face became serious because Brittany gave my arm a light shove. "You can relax. Your secret's safe with me." The next second, Baxter was grabbing Britt's hand and dragging her away to explore a specific spot in a snow berm.

It was a relief when she was gone. That warm light feeling was not to be trusted. Hopefully that emotional gooeyness was nothing more than the spirit of Christmas. If so, December twenty-sixth couldn't come soon enough.

No cars were parked in front of the third house, but the driveway was heated and led up to a three-car garage. It could easily have held the black truck, silver sedan, and tons of extra ice axes.

Britt and Baxter were a little behind me and Harper as we headed for the final driveway before we'd be crossing the road to get back to Mom's Christmas cabin. Suddenly a pair of eyes materialized from the snow. I swallowed a yell as the shape of a white furry beast broke away from its surroundings.

Instinctively I held Harper closer. "Britt," I said, forcing my voice to be low and calm, "pick up Baxter."

From Brittany's gasp, she'd also spotted the creature. Thankfully, Baxter allowed Brittany to pick him up without a fight.

What should happen next? Britt was yards away. I didn't like being so far from her, but who knew what the beast would do if I moved.

Then two things happened. One, Harper pointed at the beast and yelled, "Doggy!"

Second, a woman appeared from the final driveway and yelled, "Shaka, come!"

The creature gave a low whine before lumbering off to its owner.

A dog.

The camouflaged terror had been a dog?

I squeezed my eyes shut. The momentary relief was replaced by a feeling of foolishness. I blame Harper. If it weren't for her, I'd be wearing sunglasses and would be able to see everything much more clearly.

"Sorry about that," the woman with the beast said. "Shaka's very friendly." She was holding on to his collar as the dog strained toward Harper, who was also leaning out toward him.

"Doggy!" she said again.

This trip was going to be the death of me.

Keeping my eyes on the dog, I walked toward the duo. The woman's snow gear was athletic, and her face had the dry pinkness that came from spending a lot of time outdoors...the kind of person who could wield an ice ax.

At the crime scene, would I have noticed dog prints in the snow?

While I was distracted, Harper had wriggled down and begun petting the snow beast. The animal rolled onto his back and was unbothered when Harper toppled against him.

"How old's your daughter?" the woman asked.

"Um..." I readjusted my hat.

Should I say Harper wasn't my kid?

Nah, why bother?

Problem was, I didn't know Harper's age. If I guessed an unlikely number, I might be caught. Attempting a neighborly grin, I asked Harper, "Can you tell her how old you are?"

Harper obediently held up her hand. Since she wore mittens, we couldn't see how many fingers she held up.

The woman was delighted. "Oh, aren't you darling."

I faked a smile and nodded for the woman's benefit all while trying to look past her to the driveway.

Nothing.

It seemed this Woman with the Snow Beast's vehicle was parked in the garage.

Somehow, when I'd hatched this brilliant plan, I hadn't considered most people parked their vehicles in garages. Silly me.

Baxter had joined Harper in playing with the dog. And, to his credit, the Snow Beast had a lot more patience with children than I did.

"You arrived last night?" the woman asked as Brittany walked up.

"Yes. We got in later than intended." Britt hesitated as she thought up a reason that didn't involve a dead body. "The snow really picked up on our drive from the airport."

Britt's answer must've been too vague, because the Woman with the Snow Beast asked, "Did you see the crash? I still can't believe it. When I was on the road, it was a little dicey, but I can't believe someone died." She shook her head. "I must've just missed it."

Huh. That felt suspicious. Maybe the woman really was overly talkative, but it felt like she was trying to give herself an alibi.

Britt answered, but I didn't catch the reply.

"I hope the roads are better today," the Woman with the Snow Beast said.

I wanted to say, *Why? It's not like he died from the car crash.* But I decided it was wisest to keep my mouth shut.

During our conversation, the police car had left our house and was parked at fake Santa's brick house. For a moment I considered warning the officers to keep a close eye on the Santa impersonator, but I doubted the police would be amused.

The Woman with the Snow Beast had stiffened when the police appeared.

"Shaka."

The dog had been sprawled in the snow, tongue flopping out, with eyes rolling back as Harper and Baxter petted him. When he heard his name, he must've realized he'd been caught in an undignified moment. The joy left his eyes, and he gave a soft bark to tell the kids to get out of his way. Once there was a clear path, Shaka stood and moved to his owner.

"It's time to drive to town," the woman told the Snow Beast. "Nice to meet you all," she said with a wave. "Merry Christmas Eve."

Britt said, "Merry Christmas Eve," to the woman's retreating back.

I waited until we were out of earshot to ask, "Did you find her behavior suspicious?"

Britt raised her eyebrows. "You mean leaving her house the moment she noticed police going door to door?"

"Yeah, that."

"No. Not at all suspicious."

Then Britt winked.

I managed to keep a straight face when I said, "My bad."

We'd just returned to our driveway when Nigel and Casey's Suburban and Mom and Dad's rented SUV came driving down.

"Oh no," I muttered.

Casey and Nigel left their vehicle to retrieve their children and
harness them into car seats.

Mom unrolled her window from the SUV. "Get in," she said.

And just like that, my headache was seventeen percent worse. I
don't know why hanging out with family stresses me out so much,
but given the choice between giving a surprise presentation before my
company's board of directors in my underpants or a "family fun" trip,
I'd choose the presentation.

Britt opened the side door to show Juniper and Jude had claimed
the middle seats. It left the third row for Brittany and me. Fun fact:
the third row wasn't designed for people who are six one.

"You coming?" The annoying voice belonged to Juniper.

Blinking, I realized I was still standing by the SUV, while Brittany
was already buckled up in the back.

I raised my eyebrows at Juniper and hoped she caught my message
of *Do I have a choice?* before I got in.

"I saw that," Mom said—waiting until after Dad had the car in
drive and I was locked in.

I sighed and put on my sunglasses.

Dad was about to turn from the driveway when a black pickup
sped by. I sat up a little straighter. Which driveway had the truck come
from? And then I saw him. The white Snow Beast riding in the bed of
the truck with his tongue hanging out.

There's a chance the Woman with the Snow Beast wasn't the ax
murderer. But one thing was for sure, she'd been on the road after the
victim's car crash.

CHAPTER 7

The snow had stopped sometime in the night and the roads were clear. The wrecked vehicle was still a little ways off the road. There weren't any other signs of last night's tragedy. The snow and wind had done their job, covering up the evidence.

The sounds from the moving SUV and the six of us sitting in three different rows kept conversation to a minimum. Since Harper wasn't there, I had my sunglasses on, and Juniper had actually packed me a travel cup of coffee. I was relatively comfortable, considering my legs were crammed into a small space.

Once we got to the gas station, Dad turned in the opposite direction as the airport. Not long after, we slowed as we entered a town. In the distance were lots of brightly covered awnings and tents with rows of parked cars leading up to some ordeal.

Leaning over to the middle seat, I asked Juniper, "Are we going to a winter market?"

"The schedule says 'community center.'"

I raised an eyebrow. Was a community center worse than freezing my buns off outside?

It was Christmas Eve, and the downtown was packed with people full of holiday cheer. After some driving up and down side streets, Dad found a parking spot, but it took some doing for Casey to park and even longer for us to reconnect—especially since Harper was trying to walk while bundled up like a marshmallow.

I frowned. "Harper needs some lighter winter gear. She can't move like that." The words had been said to no one in particular, more of a grumpy statement than a conversation starter. For some reason it caught everyone's attention, and suddenly I was being stared at by nine sets of eyes.

What had I done?

Harper waddled over and reached her arms up for me to hold her. I bent down and picked her up. When I straightened, everyone was still staring.

"What?" I sounded irritated.

Suddenly everyone looked away. Even for my family, they were behaving weirdly.

Casey was the one to finally reply. "This is the first time you've had an opinion about my children."

Huh. Was that right?

"Okay," I said, because what else was there to say? Who knows how the Jacobs family decides what's a big deal. Somehow, me commenting on Harper's over-the-top snow gear made the list.

Mom quickly took charge and began leading us in the direction of the community center. Britt and I were walking in the back of the pack, when Juniper stopped and waited for me to reach her. "Brittany's a good influence," she whispered, then darted away before I could answer.

What was that supposed to mean?

"Did you hear her?" I asked.

Britt shook her head.

"Probably for the best," I muttered.

We walked on quietly, while Harper was content running a mittened hand up and down my coat's zipper. This time Harper was comfortable enough with me to let me keep the sunglasses on. Progress.

The community center's large main room had the weird smell of old building mixed with something polite people call "organic." Rows of foldout tables were filled with a variety of craft supplies with random groups of people scattered around them.

Had Mom really scheduled a crafting event? Usually, her plans involved a monument or museum. Turns out, the outside winter market would have been better. Nothing involving glitter glue.

"What's going on?" I asked, passing Harper off to Nigel.

Mom must've been full of the Christmas spirit, because instead of directing me back to the itinerary, she explained, "You mentioned Brittany's family makes homemade gifts over the holidays. I know it's not the same, but with our normal stockings in storage, I thought we could decorate new ones here."

Brittany's smile lit up her eyes as she said, "Wonderful."

Running a hand through my hair, I tried to muster up a grin. "Great," I said. And it probably was great. My mother had gone out of her way for my girlfriend, and Britt was excited. Still, couldn't Mom have done something less artsy?

Mom handed out stockings, each with our names already sewn at the top.

"You look like you're going to the dentist," Juniper said. "Will it kill you to do a craft once a year?"

I raised an eyebrow, tempted to drop a hint about my Christmas gift to Brittany. Problem was Juniper might go full interrogation. All I said was, "Trust me"—I laid my stocking down on an empty table—"I've been super crafty this year."

Brittany joined us at the table in time to hear me. She was still glowing. "You're always crafty," she said, giving me a quick kiss.

"The craftiest," Juniper said dryly.

I decided not to answer and got down to work decorating my personalized stocking. Here's the thing. I'm an engineer. What my stocking may have lacked in artistic flair, it made up for with precision.

Choosing some felt cutout stickers, I quickly had a large Christmas ornament dominating the space, with some holly around the edges to give a little pop.

I'd made my entire stocking before Juniper or Brittany had decided on their designs. At the next table, Harper's stocking was mostly globs of glitter glue smearing into each other, and she was still working.

This would take a while.

I left the group and washed up in the men's room. Not strictly necessary, but it was the best excuse I could think of to leave a room that was filling with more and more people.

I didn't rush back to the tables. Instead, I watched my family from the back wall. Britt was still beaming. Casey and Nigel were letting the kids *help* decorate their stockings. Mom was presiding over the event like an empress. And even Jude seemed to be taking his stocking assignment very seriously. This break was on borrowed time, since any second Mom or Juniper would spot me and I'd be forced to rejoin the group. Before that could happen, a group of teens trailed in with a few chaperones. The chaperones looked like...well, they looked like the type of people who'd volunteer to chaperone kids over winter vacation—a little crazy.

While I couldn't know for sure, I vaguely recognized a couple of the teens, so there was a decent chance they were the group staying in the mountain cul-de-sac.

A redheaded kid stuck out for no better reason than he had red hair.

All of them were carrying blank stockings ready to be decorated, though most of them were more focused on goofing off than pursuing artistic endeavors.

At one table, the teens were already trying to shoot glitter glue at each other. A male chaperone close to Juniper's age was trying to get a rowdier bunch of teens under control. He was fighting a losing battle, and his eyes had the vacant gaze of someone who'd been up all night. Finally, the guy just confiscated all the glue from the table and told them to decorate with stickers. The Chaperone then stood by the wall a few yards away from me—probably to cool down.

You know those times when someone's dying for a chance to talk and will take the slightest opening you give them? Well, from the way The Chaperone was side-eyeing me, I got the impression I was in one of those situations.

If I so much as blinked, I'd be getting an earful of why his day was bad.

Then it happened. A tingling in my nose that quickly spread up to my eyes.

No, no, no.

I tried to swallow it down. But it was too fast to control. My throat was already contracting, and my eyes flickered shut. My fate was sealed.

I sneezed.

Not even a loud sneeze. Yet it was the opening The Chaperone was waiting for.

"Bless you," the guy said and was standing right next to me before I got my eyes open. There wasn't even time to nod my thanks before The Chaperone was launching into a speech. "I love volunteering. It's very important for young adults to have a safe environment, since they're our next generation. But"—and he side-eyed his group to make sure no one could hear—"it's only day two and already there are a couple of kids I'd just like to"—The Chaperone held his hands in a choking position.

Excuse me?

Shouldn't he know implying you'd like to strangle children is a major faux pas? How was I stuck with him? Why wasn't Mom making me rejoin the group?

I cleared my throat, shifting a little away.

The Chaperone's ears reddened, and he dropped his hands.

Before I could mutter *bye* and leave, The Chaperone resumed talking. "Really, though, they're not so bad."

I gave a half nod. It's not like I'd believe whatever PC spin he'd attempt.

"They're hiding it, but Mr. Zeke dying last night had quite the effect on them."

Dying last night? Could this Mr. Zeke guy be the murdered man from the car accident?

I couldn't help it. My mouth opened, and I suddenly heard myself asking, "Died?"

Yikes. I'd fully engaged with the man.

I was doomed.

CHAPTER 8

"**O**h, didn't you hear?" The Chaperone's face lit up.

"Umm..."

I'd really messed up.

I know. I know. If you want to solve a murder, you might need to talk to someone unpleasant. But here's the thing—and I don't care that it's judgmental—The Chaperone was a parasite. You know the rule about not inviting a vampire into your house? Well, the same applies to people like The Chaperone. And while, yes, there is a killer to catch, I'd like to believe I can do that without selling my soul or cosigning on a timeshare.

Like seriously, the guy looked ready to dance a jig in his excitement. And this was all because I'd sneezed and then asked, *Died?*

"Most of us drove up earlier. But Zeke drove up with Wyatt a lot later than the rest of us."

Maybe I'm as ghoulish as The Chaperone. Learning there was a witness, I began scanning the teens' faces, trying to figure out which one was Wyatt.

The Chaperone was waiting for me to respond.

But I couldn't ask *What happened?* I wasn't going to feed this monster. At a certain point The Chaperone didn't know any better. But I knew better and shouldn't encourage his behavior.

Or…I wasn't going to feed the gossip monster very much. I may have given a slight nod, which was enough for him.

"After the crash, Wyatt went to get help. He found our lodge in the dark, but when we called 911, they said police were already on the scene. The police still came and talked to Wyatt. I wanted to be there, but Miss Stacy said she'd be with Wyatt when he was interviewed."

"But what about—" I began to ask before getting interrupted.

"I don't know why it was such a fuss. It's sad Zeke died in a car crash, but a vehicle accident isn't exactly breaking news."

Huh. First the Woman with the Snow Beast and now this man were both calling it an accident. In my book, there's nothing accidental about getting an ice ax to the heart. Were the police really keeping that little detail a secret?

And why hadn't Wyatt told them about the ice ax? Was the teen a murder suspect?

The Chaperone was standing right next to me, clearly hoping to get some sort of reaction. But as useful as he'd been, I didn't want to say *Thank you*. I was spared any further interaction by Harper charging at me.

"Ankle Hold! Ankle Hold!"

Casey was close behind her and said, "That's *Uncle Holt*."

"Ankle Hold!" Harper said again, jumping in front of me and raising her arms in universal kid language for *Pick me up right now*.

I gave the gossiping chaperone a curt nod, picked up Harper, and beat a swift retreat.

"Ankle Hold, can I 'ecorate your stocking like Aunt Juniper did?"

"Wait a second." I stopped a few yards away from our family's tables. "What's her name?" I pointed to Juniper.

Harper looked innocently up at me. "Aunt Juniper."

"And what's my name?"

Harper giggled. "Ankle Hold."

"Yeah, that's what I thought," I grumbled.

How come Harper was able to say *Aunt Juniper*, while I was *Ankle Hold*?

It wasn't until I reached the table and saw my stocking that I remembered the other part of what Harper had said. According to Harper, my sister had 'ecorated my stocking. But Harper couldn't read. In reality, Juniper had used glitter glue to graffiti THE BUTT under my name like it was a subtitle.

I frowned at the stocking. This was why our family shouldn't do crafts.

The glare I shot Juniper was murderous, but there was very little I could do while Harper was bouncing in my arms, saying, "See? Do you like? Do you like?"

"This isn't over," I told Juniper—though I'm not sure whether she heard with how hard she was laughing.

Harper and Baxter also started laughing, like Juniper's laughter was infectious. Pretty soon the entire family was circled around my stocking. Mom gave a half-hearted, "Juniper," but she was clearly trying to hide her smile.

How did Britt let this happen?

But Brittany was the one person still working on her stocking. Except she may not have been as innocent as it appeared at first glance. Her cheeks were slightly pinker, and her eyes were sparkling.

Wrapping my free arm around Britt, I said, "You're a lousy watchdog."

"Woof!" Harper said.

That was too much for Brittany, and silent laughter spilled out of her.

"Your boyfriend being ganged up on is funny to you?" I tried to sound annoyed, but my grin was so wide, my mouth hurt.

Brittany didn't get a chance to reply, since Mom began giving directions. "Get your stocking and bring it to whatever vehicle you rode in. We'll leave the stockings there before we head out to the next thing on the schedule."

Harper was pretty adamant I carry her while she held her stocking—something I was nervous about with all the wet glitter glue coating her creation. I prefer my black winter coat without sparkly highlights.

But I couldn't really blame Harper's need to carry her stocking. I was carrying mine in my free hand. My Christmas stocking already said, HOLT THE BUTT. Who knew what else might happen if I left it unsupervised.

For the second time, Harper let me wear sunglasses without crying. A week ago I couldn't have imagined a scenario when I wouldn't be wearing sunglasses during daylight in the snow, and now I was thankful the child I kept carrying wasn't insisting on their removal.

I don't know. Family trips are weird...and I'd thought the strangest thing would be bringing my girlfriend.

Since I was carrying Harper and I didn't trust Juniper, I brought the two of us to Casey and Nigel's vehicle. After setting my stocking in the trunk of their Suburban, I tried to figure out an easy way to remove the graffiti. Problem was, Juniper had used way less glitter glue than Harper. The glue was sort of tacky—not completely dry, but it wasn't wiping off the felt.

I took a deep breath. I wasn't sure how, but I'd get Juniper back for what she'd done.

"Do you need a moment?" Casey had come to stand beside me and was pretending to be sad about my desecrated arts-and-crafts project.

"Nope," I said. "I'm good."

Casey closed the trunk with all the stockings safely lined up inside.

I glanced at Harper. Did she still want *Ankle Hold* as her chauffeur? Since Harper wasn't paying me any attention, I figured she still wanted me to carry her and moved her to my other side. Oh, but to be clear, I work out regularly. It's not that I couldn't carry a child of her size with one arm for such a long period of time...but I didn't want to give myself an uneven workout.

I couldn't guess where we were off to next. With Mom's plans, I preferred not knowing what was in store. There was enough Christmas spirit going on around town—the next event might be a parade.

Gross.

Hopefully it wasn't a parade.

We started walking to the meet-up spot with the group from the other vehicle but didn't get very far when Casey stopped by a grocery store. "Babe," she called to Nigel, who was walking up front with Baxter.

He stopped and turned around. "What's up?"

"I forgot to pack the kids' crackers."

"Oh." Nigel checked his watch. "Is there time?"

"I'll run in with Harper. The three of you can go ahead and tell Mom."

Horror briefly flashed across Nigel's face. "What will I tell her?"

"Make Holt tell her."

"Hey!" I said.

"Or tell her it's an emergency and it's my fault," Casey said. "I'll only be a minute. Come on, princess." Casey tried to take Harper from me.

"Ankle Hold?" Harper clung to me, and her lip trembled.

I raised an eyebrow at Casey. "Mind if I join?"

Casey wasn't able to hide her surprise, but she said, "I don't mind if you don't."

"All right. Let's go, kiddo," I told Harper, and we followed my sister into the store.

It wasn't a large store by city standards, but it had around fifteen aisles with plenty of people getting groceries for Christmas dinner.

"We're looking for crackers," Casey said.

That's when Harper pointed. "Doggy!"

I expected to find a service dog, but Harper wasn't looking at a real animal. She wasn't even looking at a stuffed animal. She was pointing at a fancy helium balloon that was shaped like a spotted Christmas puppy.

"Can we check it out while you get crackers?" I asked Casey.

"Sure thing," she said, already a few yards away—clearly feeling the stress of messing with Mom's perfect schedule.

I moved to where a collection of helium balloons was floating next to the store's gift card section. Harper was content to look up and point out each new favorite balloon she discovered. I wasn't paying too much attention to my surroundings, but suddenly a hushed, overly stressed voice broke through the white noise of the grocery store.

"It's still there?" That was a man's voice.

"How did you miss it?" an equally stressed female voice said. "Yes, the wreck is still there."

Wreck? They had to be talking about last night's fatality.

"Do you think...?" The man trailed off.

"How would I know? It's snow. Got it? Snow. I can't walk up and check without leaving boot prints."

The couple was talking on the other side of the aisle, but I was in a strange L-shaped section, so maneuvering to see them was tricky. I started walking to the end of the aisle. But Harper's lip trembled, and she said, "Balloons."

This probably makes me a horrible person for prioritizing avoiding a toddler tantrum over discovering murder suspects. But after walking in the snow without sunglasses for Harper, are you really surprised I'd stay by the balloons to keep her happy?

Since I was stuck, I continued eavesdropping.

"Have the police talked to you?" the man asked.

"No," the woman said. "I left before they got to the house. Do you think they'll come back?"

"I wouldn't be surprised."

"But"—and the woman's voice grew so quiet, I almost couldn't hear—"will they be able to trace it back to us?"

Just then Harper waved her hand at her new favorite balloon, and a display of greeting cards scattered across the floor. The voices stopped.

I managed not to lose my temper as I set Harper down. She whimpered at the inconvenience of having to stand on her own two feet, but I wasn't going to attempt to pick up all the cards with their matching envelopes while squatting, one-handed, trying to keep Harper balanced in the other arm.

"Hold on," I said, trying to sound soothing.

"Doggy?" Harper asked, pointing.

But now she wasn't pointing at the balloons, but instead at the entrance to our aisle. There was the Woman with the Snow Beast...except without the Snow Beast.

Had she been the one talking?

One day Harper would be taught it was rude to point, but I'm really glad that day hadn't come.

"Oh, it's you two," the woman said, smiling—but the smile was forced. Just behind her, the figure of a man moved past, but he was too fast for me to glimpse his features.

"Doggy?" Harper asked again.

"Shaka's outside. He doesn't like shopping."

Harper nodded solemnly.

"Thanks," I said...not sure what else you're supposed to say when your miniature human starts talking to strangers.

She nodded. "Merry Christmas."

"Bye." And Harper waved—nearly knocking over more greeting cards. We had to leave this aisle as soon as I retrieved the last few envelopes, or I'd be stuck in a never-ending loop of scattered greeting cards.

Once I got the mess cleaned up, I picked Harper up and left. I don't know if she would have objected to leaving the balloons, but thankfully Harper spotted Casey.

"Mommy!"

You'd think Harper hadn't seen her mom for days, not minutes.

"Hi, sweetie." Casey beamed down at her daughter. "Did you have a nice time with Uncle Holt?"

Harper nodded.

She must be having a good time, because she still wanted me to carry her.

Casey had the crackers and we all stood in line at the checkout. I kept scanning the store for the Woman with the Snow Beast, hoping I could see the man she'd been with, but the two of them had vanished.

Once we were outside, Casey and I almost jogged to get to where the rest of the family was waiting. But this was where Harper's presence gave us a free pass. While Mom directed a frown in Casey's direction, nothing was said, and our whole group began walking toward the winter market.

We hadn't gone far when Mom came to my side. I was worried I would somehow be blamed for Casey's cracker emergency, but instead Mom smiled down at Harper. "Who's ready for some hot chocolate?"

"Meeeee!" Harper squealed and let Mom take her out of my arms.

Hot chocolate? At least it wasn't a parade.

CHAPTER 9

"Ready for more hot cocoa?" Britt asked, falling into step beside me. Her eyes were sparkling, and I knew she was thinking of our favorite sleuth from her hometown.

"Oh, you know," I said, reaching over so we could walk arm in arm. "'Tis the season for repetitive Christmas carols and hot cocoa."

"And you'll be drinking?"

"A mocha."

Britt's lips lifted in a faint smile. "Where's your Christmas spirit? You should at least get a candy cane mocha."

I grimaced. Britt was kidding, but still.

"My coffee and chocolate don't need the addition of peppermint. Thank you."

Juniper started giggling when she joined us. "What did you say to Holt? His face is green."

"None of your business," I said as Brittany replied, "Peppermint mocha."

"Uh-huh." Juniper looked between the two of us like she was missing something, then gave a quick nod before speeding up to join her husband.

Wait.

I actually stopped moving, causing Brittany to stumble since we were arm in arm. "Sorry," I said. "But...are we a couple so cringey we make Juniper uncomfortable?"

Brittany tugged at my arm, and we resumed walking. "You're overthinking this. Don't worry about it."

I sighed. Sometimes it was annoying how unfazed Brittany could be.

"But maybe?" I tried.

"Sure," Britt said. "We *might* be that cringey."

Unbelievable. Juniper was still one of the cringiest people I knew when it came to her husband. Like, they'd been married for almost a year and they still looked at each other like the other one had hung the moon.

When we reached Mom's hot cocoa shop, I was unimpressed with the windows frosted with white paint. But the interior was the real problem. The whole place was covered with an unsanitary amount of fake snow. I flinched every time one of my family members inevitably touched the fluff, full of stains from coffee spills and who knew what else.

"Hand sanitizer?" Britt had an open bottle and was hovering by my side.

"Sure," I said.

While Brittany also rubbed some on her hands, her face was the calm paramedic mask. She was taking care of me because I'd shut down in a hot cocoa shop. Fantastic.

Before I figured out a way to pretend like I wasn't bothered by the gobs of disease-ridden fake snow, Casey had joined us and was clearly on a mission. "Brittany, I have a strange question I'm dying to know the answer to."

Without a second's hesitation, Brittany said, "Yes. Holt's a very good kisser."

I tried to cover my laugh with a cough.

"Oh." Casey's mouth hung open.

Juniper had apparently been in earshot and didn't need time to recover. "Is that true?"

"Juniper"—I winked—"come on."

She rolled her eyes.

"Umm," Casey said, deciding to try again. "What I wanted to know is what's the inside of Holt's apartment like? I've imagined it as the mansion of a James Bond villain, with lots of aquariums."

"Aquariums?" I asked. "Do I look like someone who spends hours feeding fish?"

"All right," Casey said. "No fish. But...?"

"Oh, you know." Brittany's eyes flicked to mine, and I knew I was in trouble. "His kitchen's perfect, with all the right gadgets."

That wasn't so bad.

"The living room furniture coordinates with the artwork. But"—Brittany waited until both my sisters were leaning close in anticipation—"all of Holt's furniture has to pass the nap test."

I covered my face with my hands as Juniper asked, "What's that?"

"Well," Britt said. "Before Holt gets a new piece of furniture, he has to analyze it very carefully. If he can comfortably fall asleep on it, he'll buy it."

"Really?" Casey asked.

I shrugged.

"It *is* true!" Juniper squealed.

Okay, so I'd never told Brittany that. But she was right.

Really, it's my fault she figured it out. I may have fallen asleep during a few movie nights. No offense to Sandra Bullock (since she's Britt's favorite actress), but I have yet to make it through one of her chick flicks.

"Have you ever fallen asleep in a furniture store?" Juniper asked.

"Yeah, have you?" Casey asked.

"This being ganged up on"—I pointed at my sisters—"I don't love it."

"What do you love?" Juniper tilted her head toward where Britt was ordering her drink. It was definitely a challenge.

"Um..." I unzipped my jacket. The room was suffocatingly hot.

"Holt, you need to order," Mom announced.

For once Mom's timeline had saved me. I ordered my mocha, then announced, "I *love* coffee," loud enough for Juniper to hear. As good as it felt in the moment, I knew it was a bad idea. Juniper didn't respond well to taunts.

With how ordering drinks and sitting down worked out, Brittany ended up sitting by Harper and Baxter, while I was on the outskirts of the family tables. That was fine by me. The chance to brood quietly in a corner was just what I needed.

Since Juniper can't take a hint that I'm antisocial and was ready to go full hermit, she sat next to me.

"Why so glum?"

I glared at her, and Juniper reached out and tapped my nose.

"If you're not careful, your face will freeze like that."

"Give me a break," I muttered. "I just saw a dead body."

Juniper rolled her eyes. "That was last night."

I'd been about to take a sip of my mocha, but instead, I set my cup back down. "It's been under twenty-four hours."

"Fine." Juniper tossed her hair back and opened her arms melodramatically wide. "Do you want to hug and have a good weep?"

"Excuse me?" My voice was loud enough that Mom and Brittany looked over at us. Why hadn't I sat beside Nigel? At most all he'd talk about was the stock market.

"You're making a scene," Juniper whispered.

My eyes widened, but I kept my voice quiet as I said, "*You're* making the scene."

"Only because you're lying to me!"

"What?" I sat back in my chair, and my hand accidentally brushed a gob of fake snow stained tan—hopefully from apple cider.

Juniper pointed an accusatory finger in my face. "Don't think I'm fooled by your little *confused* act."

I squeezed my eyes shut. Sometimes Juniper is impossible. "It's not an act."

"You're *only* upset by last night's murder?"

I said "Yeah" but began shifting in my chair. Was she really going to interrogate me about what (or who) I loved in a crowded coffee shop?

"And you've been trying to solve the crime?" She made it sound bad.

I nodded.

"Have you told Brittany you love her?"

Even though I half expected the question, I choked and spluttered. "Juniper!"

"I'll take that as a *no*." Juniper smiled like she was proud of herself. "What are you waiting for?"

"I...Uh...*What?*"

Not a brilliant response, but I'd been ambushed.

"It's fine if you need to solve puzzles to survive family vacations. But you need to remember what's important."

I frowned. I'd forgotten just how much of a know-it-all Juniper could be.

Juniper dropped her voice so low I could barely hear. "You need to tell Britt you love her."

My only answer was "Her name's Brittany."

Instead of arguing with me about how I called my girlfriend *Britt* all the time, Juniper raised her hands up like a hostage negotiator trying to calm a kidnapper. "We all know you love Brittany. You need to say it. What are you waiting for?"

I shrugged. "It's complicated."

Juniper didn't need to hear about the Thanksgiving I'd spent with Darren. I'd asked Britt to join my family's Christmas back in September, yet she never even mentioned the option of me going to Oregon for her family's Thanksgiving.

If that's not a clue as to how your girlfriend views your relationship, I don't know what is.

"Saying *I love you* shouldn't be complicated," Juniper said. "I was talking to Casey, and she had no idea Brittany had a dead fiancé."

"Juniper"—I tried to rub the tension out of my forehead—"you shouldn't be gossiping about Britt's personal life."

My sister scrunched up her nose. "She's *your* girlfriend. It's *my* business."

I shook my head. I'd been done with this conversation before it started.

"You've never talked to me about Jeremy's death. Casey didn't know he existed. Have you ever discussed him with Brittany?"

"No!" I hadn't meant to sound upset. Trying to save the situation, I continued. "It's the worst thing that ever happened to her. I'm not going to make her relive that for me."

Juniper wasn't buying it. "Have you let her know you're willing to talk about him?"

I pulled out my phone and began checking emails.

"What, no sarcastic replies?"

I frowned.

"Why are you avoiding this?"

Who knows why I answered—maybe the spirit of Christmas. Still, I took the plunge. "She lost her fiancé, got it? Her fiancé. If he hadn't died, they'd be married and I'd be single for another Christmas."

Juniper's voice was soft. "Holt, you should talk to her." She tried to pat my hand, but I yanked it away. "It'll help, I promise."

"Sure. I'll get right on that."

Before Juniper could stick her nose further into my business, I got up, tossed my cup with mocha remnants in the trash, and stalked out of the café. I needed some air. Even if I got in trouble with Mom for abandoning the schedule, I just couldn't stay in that room any longer. Besides, there was a chance Juniper would be the one getting in trouble since it was pretty obvious she'd been trying to get a rise out of me.

Oh, and also, I don't solve crimes for the distraction. I solve them because it makes the world a safer place. And I definitely wasn't wrong for not telling Brittany I loved her. There were considerations to take into account that Juniper wouldn't understand.

I'd been striding through the Christmas town too focused on mentally yelling at Juniper to take in my surroundings. The problem with walking while angry is there's the possibility of getting lost. All of a sudden I found myself in the middle of some sort of roundabout with a ginormous decorated Christmas tree in the center. It looked more like one of Dad's Christmas puzzles than reality.

I let out a low whistle. This town certainly went all-out. How much of their annual budget was used for Christmas decor?

"It is something." Turning toward the voice, I found The Chaperone standing next to me.

Seriously, this guy was the worst.

The only thing he'd be good for was telling me which teen had been in the car crash. But I couldn't ask him. The guy would definitely tell me, but then I'd be a ghoul just like him.

Still...I was trying to catch a murderer. Would it be all right if he happened to bring it up?

I started with "Where are the kids?"

The Chaperone looked momentarily excited before remembering his mask of patient long-suffering. "They're trying to play Frisbee in the snow." He gestured behind us, where the teens were in a small park attempting to catch and throw an orange Frisbee while wearing gloves.

These kids were playing Frisbee in the snow on Christmas Eve.

"Hold on," I said, a new question taking shape. "Why are you on a youth trip over Christmas? Shouldn't the kids be with their families?"

Why had I asked that? It's not like I cared. Still, it was odd that parents would ship their kids off for such a family-oriented holiday.

The Chaperone said, "Good question. Good question."

Was it a good question?

"Usually, the winter trip happens over New Year, but there was a booking problem. We didn't know if it'd work out. But people were unexpectedly on board. Some of the parents went on a humanitarian trip over Christmas. And some of the families are complicated. Like Gracie's parents are mid-divorce, and it was a relief to send her somewhere drama-free."

I raised an eyebrow. A murder wasn't exactly *drama-free*.

One kid ran for the disc, and as he sped up, I noticed he was limping. Had he been in the crash?

"Is he all right?" I asked, since I'm a thoughtful and caring person—not because I'm an armchair detective.

"What? Oh." The Chaperone for some reason sounded disappointed. "Yeah. He messed up his knee snowboarding last week." The Chaperone shrugged. "Pete's fine."

If only Juniper were here. She'd get The Chaperone to tell her everything, and she wouldn't feel guilty for doing it.

I knew I shouldn't ask who had been in the car with the murder victim. It felt morally wrong to ask. But when had that stopped me? If Santa was giving me coal anyway, did it really matter if I meddled a little more?

"So the kid in the crash last night wasn't injured?"

"Wyatt? Yeah, he's good."

I was figuring out a nonpredatory way of asking which one was Wyatt when The Chaperone made the mortifying decision of yelling, "Hey, Wyatt, this guy wants to talk to you about last night."

The redhead I'd noticed from the community center threw the Frisbee and turned to face us. The teen's eyes widened. Before I could wonder at the scared face, Wyatt bolted.

It made sense. Wyatt had been choosing between fight or flight.

Flight had definitely won.

If I were by myself, I wouldn't have followed. Adult men chasing after kids are featured on the news in a very negative light. Thing is, I wasn't alone. I was with a no-good chaperone.

"Look what you've done!" the guy shouted—apparently the spooked kid was somehow my fault. "After him!" The Chaperone was already panting and hadn't moved five feet. "Come on," he said, when I still hadn't moved. "I can't misplace another kid."

I raised an eyebrow. Just how many kids had he lost track of?

"Please," The Chaperone called, attempting to run but getting nowhere fast.

Ordinarily, I wouldn't have been pressured into stalking a teen through a winter market, but this time the teen had information I wanted. Besides, with The Chaperone's blessing, it was unlikely I'd end up on the nightly news.

I easily outdistanced The Chaperone and caught a streak of red hair as he turned into what I can only assume was an alley.

Not great. As a general rule, I avoid strange alleys for safety reasons. This town might look like a Thomas Kinkade painting, but that didn't mean shady stuff wasn't happening in dark alleyways.

When I reached the turn, it was creepier than I'd expected. It almost resembled a bizarre funhouse. There was a row of dumpsters all decorated with Christmas lights. I shuddered. It had to be from some city ordinance. No way any normal person cared enough to put twinkle lights on trash containers.

"I know you're here," I called, holding my palms out in front of me, doing my best to look nonthreatening.

What was it police had to do? Identify themselves as law enforcement? I needed to introduce myself. "My name is Holt Jacobs. What's your name?"

I think I've seen a hostage negotiator in a movie ask for a name, so it was strategic...not because I'd already forgotten it.

When the only answer I got was silence, I said, "I was there last night." I moved slowly into the alley. "I just want to talk about what you saw."

Turns out that was a bad thing to say. Suddenly a bag of trash was getting chucked at me, and the teen was racing down the alley.

"Wait!" I yelled, sidestepping the garbage and resuming the chase.

Who did he think I was, the killer?

"Your chaperone is really worried," I tried.

That didn't work. I had a major problem. Was there anything I could say that would make the kid stop and talk to me?

While I'm a regular at the gym, I'm no longer sixteen and track was never a passion of mine. I'd managed to keep within eyesight of the redhead as he turned from alley to street, to side street, but the distance was slowly growing and there was nothing I could think of to say to get the teen to trust me.

Then a miracle happened. A little ways ahead, the redhead slipped and tumbled to the ground.

This was my chance. Giving one final burst of speed, I made it there just as the teen was righting himself.

"Please," I wheezed—more out of breath than I'd realized.

For a second I thought he'd stay. Then his eyes hardened, and he was running again.

As I moved forward to continue the chase, my shoe slid on the same patch of ice the teen had slipped on. My arms waved frantically, and I swallowed a yell as my feet gave out from under me and I crash-landed onto my backside.

At first my world shrank to pain and humiliation, but when I was able to focus, Juniper stood in front of me, arms crossed and hip popped.

She shook her head. "You clearly didn't run track in high school."

CHAPTER 10

J uniper was arguably the worst person to watch me fall. I was
sprawled on the cement, my butt a painful sort of numb, and all I
got from my sister was a snarky comment.

"What are you doing here?" I growled.

"Mom made me go hunting for you." To her credit, Juniper did
offer me a hand up. "She told me I needed to apologize for whatever I
said that made you so mad."

When I got to my feet, I wasn't quite ready to stand and ended up
leaning against a fire hydrant.

"And?" I asked, trying to rub the small of my back through my
jacket.

Juniper tilted her head. "*And* I found you. Let's go."

My sister had the sort of confidence that meant she had walked a
few yards before she noticed I was still leaning against the fire hydrant.

I grinned. "I'm waiting."

Juniper wrinkled her nose. "For what?"

"That apology."

Juniper rolled her eyes. "You can't be serious."

I raised an eyebrow. "Do I look like I'm kidding?"

"Well, I'm not sorry. You should tell Brittany you love her right
away before she gets bored and dumps you."

My mouth twitched, and it took work to act like I wasn't bothered. "Wow, sis." I forced a laugh. "You're really bad at apologizing."

The huff of air Juniper exhaled was made extra dramatic since it puffed a cloud of frozen mist into the air. "What are you even doing here?" she asked.

I decided to go with the truth since I was curious what Juniper would do with it. Looking her dead in the eye, I said, "I'm chasing a redheaded boy."

"Umm..." Juniper tapped one gloved finger to her lip, and then her eyes lit up at something behind me. "Do you mean him?"

Twisting around, I saw the teen I'd been chasing watching me from under the awning of an antique store. "Yeah. He's the guy," I said.

The teen stiffened when our eyes met, and I knew if I moved an inch, he'd bolt.

Good thing I had a secret weapon.

"Juniper, if you get that kid to talk to me, we're good."

"Cool," Juniper said, already wearing her dazzling influencer smile as she approached the teen. I couldn't hear what she said, but whatever Juniper's siren song was, it definitely charmed teenage boys.

When Juniper returned, he was following, and my sister made a formal introduction. "Wyatt, this is my brother, Holt. He has a few questions for you."

Wyatt was more focused on his shoes than on me, but Juniper had gotten him here. I decided to start with an easy question. "Why did you stick around?"

He shrugged. "You screamed so loud when you fell, I wanted to see if you broke a hip."

I bit my tongue to keep from answering. First off, I'd made sure to keep all my yelling on the inside. Second off, "How old do you think I am?"

(At least I kept part of it to myself.)

"I dunno." Wyatt smirked. "Real old. Maybe fifty."

Fifty?

"Fifty!"

"Be nice," Juniper said, but I wasn't sure if she was talking to me or the teen.

I'd been about to tell Wyatt that I was thirty, yet for once my sister may have had a point. I sighed. Somehow I'd pictured this going smoother.

I said, "Fine," and I let the debate about my advanced years drop. "Your chaperone said you were in the car last night when it crashed?"

"So?" Wyatt tried to punctuate the word with the overconfidence teens use when speaking to adults, but there was fear in his eyes.

I could do this. I could talk to an arrogant teenager without losing my temper.

I said, "*So*, can you tell me what happened?"

"No," he said.

I glared at Juniper. "You sent me a hostile witness."

Juniper scrunched up her nose. We both knew I'd take back our deal if I didn't get the information I wanted.

"Remember what we talked about?" Juniper's voice had a bewitching sound that I'd *almost* grown immune to.

Wyatt looked at my sister. He straightened his shoulders and fixed his coat.

Juniper nodded. "Tell him what you know."

The teen's expression soured as he refocused on me. "Whatever," he said. Then, to prove how mundane he found the whole affair, Wyatt yawned so wide, I saw his tonsils—I would have preferred not seeing his tonsils, but if yawning somehow made him ready to talk, I'd put up with it.

"The reason I can't tell you what happened," Wyatt finally said, "is because I don't know. I was asleep."

Huh. Not what I'd expected.

My sister couldn't quite suppress her giggle. "That sounds like you."

I frowned. "Not helping."

Wyatt smirked at our exchange, and I forced myself to hide my irritation. If I were more official, I could be speaking with a witness in a heated office or an interrogation room, instead of leaning against a fire hydrant in freezing temperatures with a bruised behind and a giggling sister.

"Why don't you tell me what you remember?" I asked, trying to sound like I knew what I was doing.

Wyatt looked over at Juniper before shrugging. "Uh, I had this big presentation thing after school. Mr. Zeke picked me up and drove us from Bozeman after the rest of the group left." Wyatt stopped talking, and it seemed like he thought he'd shared everything I'd want to know.

Before I could say anything, Juniper nodded encouragingly and said, "And?"

For the first time, a flicker of annoyance flashed across Wyatt's face as he looked at her.

"I dunno. I was sleeping in the car, and then there was a crash. When I woke up, the car was in a ditch and Mr. Zeke was slumped over the steering wheel. I couldn't get him to wake up and there was no cell service, but his phone's GPS was still on and I saw how close we were to the lodge, so I walked over to get help."

Hold on. According to Wyatt, the ax victim had been slumped against the steering wheel when he'd left. Then what about the ice ax? Since the police were leaving that tiny detail a secret, I didn't want to ask directly.

Though technically this kid could be the killer, somewhere under all the layers of arrogance was a person who'd walked on a dark mountain road during a snowstorm to get help. If Wyatt didn't know anything about the ice ax, I didn't want to traumatize him unnecessarily. I'd have to take a roundabout approach.

"Did you take any weapons to defend yourself from...bears?"

"Bears?" The way the teen said the word made it clear I was the dumbest person he'd ever met. "I don't know if your first-grade teacher ever told you this, but bears hibernate when it's cold out."

This time Juniper didn't even try to hide her giggle.

Taking off my hat, I smoothed back my hair. This was what some teenagers do—try to get a rise out of adults. If I wanted Wyatt's full story, I'd have to play along.

"Right," I said. "Not bears because they hibernate. But did you really walk alone at night with nothing to protect you?"

"Uh, yeah." Wyatt sounded disappointed with my mature answer. "What would I have grabbed? Mr. Zeke's ice ax?"

Say what?

While I was still processing the words, Juniper was practically jumping up and down as she asked, "Mr. Zeke brought an ice ax?"

"Yeah." And then—since Wyatt had to behave like a stinker—he added, "I just said that."

"But why would he even bring one?" I asked.

"I think it was a gift for someone he knew up here."

Juniper and I looked at each other. Mr. Zeke had friends here? People who could have wanted him dead? That solved one tiny piece of the puzzle. It wasn't a motive, but it made a lot more sense if the killer knew him.

Still, imagine the bad luck of packing the weapon someone would murder you with.

Before I could think of a polite way to tell Wyatt I was out of questions and he could get lost, Juniper asked, "Did anybody ask if you needed help when they drove past you on the road?"

"Oh." Wyatt's attention shifted back to his shoes. "They kind of didn't see me."

"Why's that?" Juniper and I asked in unison.

A pink that wasn't from the cold crept up Wyatt's cheeks. "You know...because I hid behind the trees...Stranger danger."

"Right," I said.

I may have grinned at knowing Wyatt was actually scared walking through the woods at night after pretending so hard that he was fearless.

"Can I go now?"

"Sure thing," I said.

Wyatt vanished before I could say thank you...or tell him to go back to his chaperone.

"Well," Juniper said, standing right beside me.

"Well?"

"Time to go." She grabbed my arms and tried to pull me upright. I didn't budge. "Holt, come on. A deal's a deal."

Crossing my arms, I said, "It's hard to walk with a broken butt."

"Broken? It's probably not even bruised."

I raised an eyebrow, but she was right. My backside was no longer on fire—though it was pretty numb from sitting too long on a frozen fire hydrant.

Juniper inhaled loudly to let me know how much of an inconvenience I was, before stooping down and slinging my arm over her shoulder. "Come on, big guy."

Originally I'd planned on leaning against Juniper just enough to make her grumble, but as I stood, I found my legs were more numb than I realized, and we both stumbled.

"Holt!"

"Sorry," I said, shaking free of Juniper. If I went down, I wasn't taking her with me. I slipped and slid but was able to stay upright as blood flow returned.

When we reached my parents' rental car, Mom was waiting outside, while Britt, Jude, and Dad sat in the warmth of the SUV.

Mom leveled Juniper with a parental glare. "Did you apologize?"

Under normal circumstances I would have loved to watch Juniper squirm. As it was, I really didn't want Juniper explaining what she'd done to make me storm off. There was no way I wanted Mom weighing in on whether I should tell Brittany I loved her. Plus, the conversation would have taken place with Brittany sitting in the SUV possibly overhearing everything.

Before Juniper answered, I said, "We're good," and climbed inside.

Britt was waiting for me in the back seat.

"Hey," I said.

She didn't answer and instead was looking me over with her professional paramedic face. "What happened?" she asked.

I shrugged. "Sorry for ditching."

CHAPTER 11

Not wanting her to keep analyzing my face, I rested my head on top of hers.

And there I was being a bad boyfriend who emotionally shut down. It's not like Brittany was buying me resting my head as being tired. My whole body was rigid, so it was pretty clear I wasn't about to drift off.

Brittany set her hand on my knee but otherwise let me be.

I sighed. Maybe I did need a nap. Somehow I was overcomplicating things.

But was explaining to Brittany about my little fight with Juniper in a car full of people really a good option? And what if I took Juniper's advice? The first time I said *I love you* wouldn't be in front of my mommy.

A little way out of town, Juniper twisted to face us. "You know what's next on the schedule?"

"No," I said, glad for an excuse to sit up. My body was too tense for such a relaxed position leaning against Britt.

"We'll be having sandwiches for lunch," Brittany said, not even glancing at me.

Was Britt mad?

"Yeah, sandwiches." Juniper waved her hand like it was inconsequential. "But before lunch, Holt, do you know what you're doing?"

"No, Juniper. I obviously have no idea what I'm doing."

Dad cleared his throat at the steering wheel...There's a chance my voice was louder than appropriate for an enclosed vehicle. Which meant everyone knew for certain that I was in a bad mood. Fantastic.

"What were you saying?" Brittany asked Juniper—but her voice was too controlled, too polite. It wasn't Britt, but her professional self. This was bad.

"Oh." Juniper was still twisting awkwardly in her seat and looked from me to Britt. "Um, I was just making sure Holt knew his mother-child bonding session was coming up." She bit her lip, almost looking guilty for piling on problems, and rushed through the last sentence. "You're making gingerbread."

I stared at her blankly. "Casey just made gingerbread."

"She rolled gingerbread cookies with Mom. You'll be making the loaves." When I didn't even flinch with this update, Juniper whispered something in Jude's ear, and he nodded.

I bowed my head in my hands and pretended I was alone.

With all the stress involved with bringing my girlfriend on a family vacation, I'd forgotten about Mom's mandatory bonding sessions. It was a tradition Mom enjoyed a lot more than I did. Especially since *bonding* was code for *interrogation*.

The car slowed down before gradually stopping. In front of us was a large white passenger van with its brake lights glowing. What was going on?

I crowded into Britt's space to look through the windshield. Past the van was a tow truck and a police car in the process of attaching the wrecked vehicle to the tow truck.

That had to happen now? I didn't mean to let my breath out in a huff—but what were the chances I'd be stuck in a traffic jam in the middle of the Montana mountains?

As we waited, a second passenger van pulled up behind us, followed by Casey and Nigel's Suburban. I shifted until my face was pressed up against the passenger window as I tried to watch the wreck get pulled onto the truck.

I was so focused on that, I almost missed something that could be an actual clue. There were paw prints in the snow. Now, with me being more of a city boy and sitting in the back seat of an SUV at a strange angle, I couldn't be sure they were dog prints...They may have been moose prints and I wouldn't have known the difference.

Still, had the Snow Beast walked around the murder scene with his owner? When I'd overheard the Woman with the Snow Beast in the store, I thought she said she couldn't examine the wreck because of the snow. Had she lied? And what were she and the man she was talking to so afraid of?

These questions were puzzling enough that I didn't notice when the tow truck and police car drove away. I didn't even notice that we'd started moving again. It was a surprise when Dad had parked and we were back at the lodge.

I didn't go immediately inside and instead dawdled by the SUV, taking my chance for a few seconds of quiet. Mom had said we'd get to baking in fifteen minutes, which was hardly any time to decompress.

My bedroom was the kitchen pantry, where my only seating option was an air mattress and there'd be plenty of interruptions as Casey or Nigel popped in to grab snacks for their kids.

I may have hidden behind the car when Nigel's Suburban came up the driveway. It was definitely creepy lurking in the shadows as Casey and Nigel unloaded their kids, but talking to anyone in a reasonable way was unlikely, so I stayed put.

Once Harper and Baxter were out of their car seats, the whole gang trooped around to the trunk and took out their stockings.

Two things happened at once. First, Nigel bent to get my stocking and a Sharpie fell out of his coat pocket. Second, Juniper's glitter-glue inscription of THE BUTT sparkled for a moment in the sunshine before Nigel headed into the house.

I waited outside long enough for everyone to get their snow gear off, then picked up Nigel's abandoned Sharpie and snuck inside.

The living room was empty, though sounds of family echoed from the kitchen and upstairs. The aesthetic fireplace was now crammed with ten homemade stockings.

What I needed to do would take only a few seconds. Still, I double-checked the coast was clear before striding across the room, uncapping the marker, and writing THE BRAT on Juniper's stocking under her name.

"What are you doing?" Harper's voice surprised me as I was drawing the top bar of the *t*, and the line slanted unusually low.

My jaw ticked. This was less artsy than Juniper's, but it got the point across.

"Ankle Hold?"

Harper was waiting. What was the appropriate answer for a toddler? Forcing a smile, I said, "It's a surprise for Aunt Juniper."

Harper didn't respond. She only stood watching me with big innocent eyes. I shifted on my feet, not allowing myself to feel guilty for getting back at Juniper. Still, Harper kept watching.

"Why don't you go tell her?" I said.

Harper thought it over before saying "Okay" and wandering off.

I collapsed onto the recliner with a sigh. That wouldn't buy much time, and once Juniper arrived, there'd be no quiet, but I'd earned myself a few seconds of peace.

I unlocked my phone and was scrolling aimlessly when I remembered the video I'd filmed of the crime scene.

Wyatt had said he was the only other person in the car, and when he'd left, the victim had been unconscious at the wheel. If that were true, Wyatt's tracks would be the least visible of the three sets. And his footprints would lead away from the crash. Was there a way to see if he'd told the truth from what I'd filmed?

I began playing the video in slow motion. Even with the best phone on the market, it was still hard to pick up details of shoe size or tread. Watching the video was also strangely calming. I shouldn't be fighting a yawn as the image of a man with an ice ax in his heart appeared, but *shouldn't* and *didn't* are two very different things.

Turning up the brightness, I squinted at the markings in the snow. Could the human eye really pick out any clues? Maybe this was the job of a fancy computer algorithm that cop shows are always using.

Harper surprised me again when she suddenly stood in front of me. "I couldn't find her," she said, shaking her head dramatically from side to side.

"Thanks for checking."

I expected Harper to leave, but instead she climbed into my lap. I put away my phone—even I know watching raw footage of a crime scene with a child is a bad idea.

Now what? In a few minutes Mom would be marching in and making me bake gingerbread with her. How was I supposed to mentally prepare with a miniature human sitting on me?

Harper set her head on my chest and positively melted against me. Somehow my head began resting against the recliner, and I was yawning again. Keeping my eyes open with this little radiator was proving impossible. The way Harper was settled on me was like a weighted blanket.

Gingerbread and sandwiches could wait. The only question was, could Mom?

CHAPTER 12

I woke up to a hand clawing at my throat. On instinct, I pushed the hand away.

"Ankle Hold?"

I opened my eyes too quickly, and at first all I could see was a blob on my lap. It took a few seconds of blinking before Harper came into focus. From her mussed hair and the red mark on her cheek, she'd also just woken up.

Harper stretched, and for the second time her hand was at my throat.

"Stop it," I said, batting her hand away. When Harper heard my extra gravelly voice, she giggled and ran away.

I attempted to fix my hair. Even without checking the time, I knew I'd missed lunch, and based on the smell, gingerbread had been baked without me. While I was hungry, I was tempted to fall back to sleep. Problem was, with Harper gone, Mom would wake me up for whatever event was scheduled.

Also, I'd been a pretty bad boyfriend. First I'd abandoned Britt when I stormed out of the café, then I was distant on the drive, and now I'd taken an accidental nap. I had to find her, but before I did anything, I needed coffee.

Somehow I managed to go from the living room, through the dining room, and to the kitchen without being noticed...or so I thought.

I was halfway through refilling my travel cup when Juniper's "What are you doing?" caused coffee to slosh over my hand. She sat on the counter by the oven, swinging her legs back and forth. Jude was also seated on the counter, one arm wrapped around my sister, the other holding his phone.

My only answer was to frown, then finish filling up my travel cup.

Juniper abandoned her perch to stand beside me. "You look awful." She seemed equal parts amused and concerned. "Here." Juniper went to the fridge and pulled out a plate. "We made you a sandwich."

I sat on a barstool and yawned before asking, "Who made the sandwich?"

"Does it matter?" Juniper set the plate in front of me.

A quick inspection under the bread showed a reasonable amount of meat, cheese, and mayo, but I remained suspicious. "I've already had one of your peanut butter sandwiches this year. It was a gloopy mess. I'm not eating another one of your concoctions."

Jude looked up from his phone but didn't comment.

My sister rolled her eyes. "I can't believe you remember that."

"It was pretty memorable."

The kitchen timer began beeping as Juniper said, "Eat the sandwich. Don't eat the sandwich. I'm not telling you who made it."

I ate the sandwich.

Mom's voice could be heard in the distance as I refilled my coffee.

"Oh, since you were like this"—Juniper shoved her phone in my face with a photo of me and Harper asleep on the recliner—"Mom made me bake gingerbread with her, which means you'll be wrapping presents."

I groaned. What was worse? The fact that Juniper had baked something or that I was supposed to wrap a million gifts?

Bonding with Mom while baking at least involved the science of food chemistry. Plus, who knew if Juniper's gingerbread would even be edible. She couldn't make a peanut butter sandwich. Could she be trusted to use an oven?

"Are you getting sick?" Juniper put her hand on my forehead like she'd be able to tell from that. "Maybe Brittany should check on you."

Brittany. Where was Brittany?

Before I could ask, Mom barged into the kitchen. "Good, you're awake." Then, without pausing, she added, "Let's go. There's lots of gifts to wrap before we have to go outside again."

I think I tried to smile. But all that happened was a locked jaw.

"Tell Britt I said hi," I told Juniper as Mom dragged me away.

But Mom had only brought me to the dining room when Nigel appeared. He smiled at Mom and asked, "Could I have a minute alone with Holt?"

If I'd tried something like that, Mom would never have gone along with it. But since it was her son-in-law asking for a favor, Mom said, "Of course. I'll be waiting in the living room."

Then, just like that, Mom left.

I was too surprised by Mom postponing our bonding session to wonder what Nigel wanted.

"Is my family in danger?" he asked.

My head snapped up to meet his. "Excuse me?"

What was he talking about?

Nigel took a step closer and lowered his voice. "The police were here this morning. But you didn't have to talk to them, because you spoke with them last night. They had all sorts of questions but said they were just following up on a *car accident*."

"There's no need for you to worry," I said. "Nothing bad will happen to your family."

"Sorry, Holt, but that's not good enough. In May there was all this criminal stuff going on that I didn't know about, and then suddenly you were in the hospital."

"That was months ago," I said, trying to ease past Nigel. "And Casey knew."

Nigel held up his hand. "Whatever. Forget about last May. Today, when we drove past the wrecked car, I got a good look at it. From the damage, I'd guess no one actually died in the crash. Also, police don't go door to door asking if anyone's seen anything when the cause of death is an icy road."

"Right," I said, wondering how I could get around him and escape to the living room, where Mom would be waiting to take me upstairs.

"You can tell him." This voice came from behind me, and I snapped around to find Jude had snuck up on us.

"You know what happened?" Nigel asked him.

Jude's fingers twitched liked he wanted to hide behind his phone, but he nodded. "Juniper told me last night."

"Of course Juniper knew." Nigel shook his head. "Somehow Holt tells one sister everything and the other sister nothing."

"To be fair"—there may have been a twinkle in Jude's eyes—"Holt doesn't have much choice when it comes to Juniper. She's very...persuasive."

"Sure," Nigel said.

There was a silence during which I was probably expected to tell Nigel everything I knew. But I didn't. This may have been juvenile stubbornness, but I didn't appreciate being ambushed ten minutes after I'd woken up.

"Well, Holt?" Jude had his arms crossed, and he was watching me.

I nodded—though it wasn't like I needed Jude's permission. "The car crashed. Then, sometime after that, the driver was murdered."

"Okay," Nigel said. "Thank you for letting me know."

At first I didn't answer. Saying *I didn't have a choice* could come across as bitter. But I was almost to the living room when I turned back to Nigel. "Seriously, man. Don't worry about it. Nothing bad will happen to your family. I promise."

Promising may have been a bit extreme. It's not like I actually knew the future. But this murder didn't seem to relate in any way to Nigel or his family.

Mom was waiting near the stockings and led me to her bedroom on the second floor. Two card tables were set up. On one rested lots of wrapping paper, ribbons, tape, and scissors, while the other table had a partially completed one-thousand-piece puzzle with Dad sitting next to it.

If Michael Bublé's music was Mom's Christmas tradition, working on jigsaw puzzles was Dad's.

I've been known to work on a puzzle from time to time, and I gave a low whistle when I saw the picture on the box. Dad was working on a fantastical ice crystal castle. All the pieces were similar shades of light blues and grays.

While Dad was sitting by the jigsaw, he'd been reading a very big book instead of putting pieces together.

"Giving up?" I asked.

Dad added a bookmark, then closed his book. "Never. My eyes just needed a break." Only Dad would think resting his eyes meant reading.

Dad set the book on the table with a relaxed smile. "Sit down. Your mom's not quite ready." Dad's a natural. He gave a very convincing performance. But there was a rustle behind me, and I caught Mom mid–sign language.

When our eyes met, Mom left the room.

Ugh.

The only thing worse than having a meltdown in front of family is how they behave after.

"Come on." Dad tilted his head to an empty chair that just so happened to be next to the puzzle table instead of the gift-wrapping station.

It was pretty fishy.

Would Mom pretend gift-wrapping was scheduled and then pull a switch?

The answer was yes.

Absolutely.

It was surprising she hadn't pulled a stunt like this before.

My eyes locked with Dad's. "This is a setup."

Dad's eyes crinkled, but that was the only giveaway. Picking up the puzzle box, he said, "You see how the gargoyles are more sandstone? Can you find me those pieces?"

"Sure." I managed to keep my thoughts to myself for a good long while, but being ambushed by Dad was too bizarre to let go. "Why is Mom making us hang out?" Thankfully, Dad knows me well enough that he wasn't offended by the question.

"She thought you could use"—he cleared his throat—"uh, dating advice."

I snorted. "Nope. I'm good. Trust me, Juniper's already given me plenty of advice."

"That's what we're afraid of." The dryness in Dad's voice caught my attention. The lines on his face had tightened. He was serious.

Did everyone think I was in danger of wrecking my relationship? Smoothing back my hair, all I could say was, "Dad..."

He nodded and almost looked relieved. "I'll mind my own business."

Had Mom really expected the two of us to have a deep heart-to-heart?

Then Dad asked, "What's going on with your mystery?"

I raised an eyebrow. "This is minding your own business?"

Dad winked.

What was going on?

In general Dad and I don't chat. Was he still working for Mom? But his eyes were bright, and his fingers were tapping the thick book in front of him. The picture on the cover was of a pipe and one of those old-fashioned hats with all the folds on it.

"You're reading Sherlock Holmes!" I accused.

Dad shrugged. "Your point is? What's wrong with wanting to take on the role of Dr. Watson in my son's life?" His voice changed, becoming deeper and a little slower. *"For the longest time I've held the strongest fascination for the peculiar insights of my eldest child, Holt Jacobs."*

"Dad!" Sure it was all a joke, but I felt heat rising up my face. "You've been around other mysteries."

"I know." For a moment Dad almost resumed being the bookish professor we all knew and loved. Then the battle was lost and he was leaning out of his chair looking an awful lot like Baxter begging for a second piece of candy. "But it's snow. A snow murder. Do you know how rare that is? Sherlock will walk backward in snow or hide unnoticed until the snow is too trampled down to spot individual boot prints. Do you think that happened?"

"Umm..." There were no words. Blame it on not drinking enough coffee, but I handed Dad my phone with the crime scene video playing and absolutely no warning. He grunted at one point—probably when it showed the dead body.

Dad could come up with his own conclusions, but I doubted someone would walk backward in the snow after committing murder on the side of the road with an ice ax.

Mom returned at that moment with a cup of coffee. "Time to work," she said, giving me the mug.

I moved my chair to Mom's gift-wrapping table, and she began going through a lengthy list of presentation expectations. At one point I literally had to raise my right hand and solemnly swear that I wouldn't tell anyone what the gifts were.

Finally I was able to get to work. I really needed to check in with Brittany, and the sooner the presents were wrapped, the sooner I could leave. While Juniper may have created more artistic gift-wrapping displays, no one is more precise than an engineer on a mission.

I was so focused on taping perfect lines, I didn't notice Mom's lack of interrogation and almost missed another round of hand signals to Dad.

But I did see and then rolled my eyes. "Yes, Mom, we talked. I wept. Happy?"

Mom pressed her lips together into a tight line—seconds later Dad had Sherlock Holmes open so he could pretend not to hear.

But Mom didn't say anything, just continued adding bows and ribbons with rigid shoulders. Two could play that game. Also, I was a lot better at sitting in silence than Mom was.

With no chitchat slowing me down, I finished wrapping all the gifts in record time. It wasn't that I enjoyed Mom's radiating displeasure, but a lifetime of experience had taught me I was guaranteed to lose any argument we got into.

After cleaning up the little shreds of wrapping paper from my workstation, I was going to leave and congratulate myself on a bonding session mostly free from prying, when Mom took my hand.

"I think Brittany is really good for you."

"Okay."

Instinctively, I pulled my hand away.

"Holt"—Mom waited until I looked her in the eye—"and you're good for her."

My jaw ticked and I tried to answer, but it felt like my throat had swollen. "I don't know...I..." Then I shrugged.

A faint smile played across Mom's face, and she glanced over at Dad reading Sherlock Holmes. "You know"—Mom almost blushed—"if someone better than you chooses you, just go with it."

"Right. Uh...thanks."

Not wanting any more advice, I turned and left.

I was stuck. I knew how I felt about Brittany, but I also knew she didn't feel it back. Turning to the stairs, I almost collided with Britt on her way down from the third floor.

"I love you," I blurted without thinking. Our eyes widened, and I took a step back. Britt grabbed my arm before I could take another step—probably for the best since I'd forgotten the stairs were behind me.

"Did you say...?" Brittany's face was unreadable, and her eyes were almost harsh as she scrutinized my face.

"What? No. I mean, yes." I rested an arm against the wall, suddenly feeling lightheaded. "Sorry about today. This all started because Juniper told me I needed to tell you I love you, and then people kept trying to weigh in."

Britt's scar was outlined, and she was using her professional voice when she said, "I don't want you to be pressured into saying something you don't feel."

Wait...what?

"Don't feel?" My voice cracked. "Don't feel! Of course I love you. I've loved you since..." I actually couldn't think of a time I hadn't loved her. I took a deep breath. This was coming out all wrong. "I love you, but I never said it so you wouldn't be obligated to say it back." Raking a hand through my hair, I couldn't quite meet Britt's eyes.

"Why would I be obligated to say it?"

"Britt"—I shifted and for the second time nearly tumbled down the stairs—"it doesn't matter."

Brittany grabbed me by the shoulders, her grip surprisingly strong. "It matters."

I closed my eyes. This conversation was the exact thing I'd been trying to avoid. Somewhere downstairs Chouzie barked.

Brittany muttered something under her breath before taking my hand and leading me upstairs to her bedroom. Once I was seated on the mattress, she knelt in front of me. "You look like you're about to pass out. Are you dizzy?"

"Yeah," I said, closing my eyes and rubbing my temples.

"Too bad."

My eyes popped open. Had she just said that?

But Britt wasn't done. "Time to tell me what's going on. If you faint, you'll land on the mattress. There's no point in me saying 'I love you, too' if you don't believe me."

"Britt..." I shook my head. "Please, I might throw up."

Apparently that was all the permission my body needed, and I gagged. Brittany moved the trash can closer but still expected me to spell out the obvious.

"Holt?" Worry had crept into her voice. "What's going on?"

I had the sweats, was about to puke and then faint. Was saying *I love you* usually so stressful?

"Holt, please."

Sighing, I tried to pull myself together. Managing a grin, I said, "It's fine," and stood up. Brittany also stood and might have blocked my way if I'd gone for the door.

I shook my head. "You're not supposed to be with me," I said. "If things had gone the way they should have, you'd be married to a hunky coast guard, not dating my whiny butt." I cleared my throat, and there was an abnormal amount of liquid in my eyes. "It's fine. I don't mind being an escape or a runner-up if that means I get to date you."

The scar by Britt's eyebrow was even more defined, and she still seemed confused. "And what's wrong with saying 'I love you'?"

"If all I am is a fun distraction, me loving you is too much and you'll dump me."

"You're afraid because you love me, I'll dump you on Christmas?"

Something in her voice made me really look at her. Brittany's eyes were dancing.

"Do you find this *funny*?!"

"Well..." Brittany covered her mouth. "Sort of."

"Wow. Okay," I said. "Thanks, by the way. Really glad I opened up."

"Will you shut up!" Brittany closed the distance between us and cupped my jaw in her hand. "Listen to me. I really liked Jeremy. My mom and Paul told me how great he was. When he proposed, I never had a second thought about saying yes."

I grimaced, and my stomach gave a sickening flip. "Britt, stop. Please."

But she didn't. "I really liked Jeremy. I was devastated when he died. Sometimes after it happened, I could hear all the supportive things he'd say about how brave and courageous I was. But"—Britt bit her lip—"when we started dating, I knew if you could send me a message from beyond the grave, it would be to complain about all the harp music in heaven."

Brittany laughed, but I didn't see the joke. My knees were beginning to buckle, and my vision was blurry enough, I wasn't confident I could sit on the bed.

"Holt," Britt said. "Do you understand?"

"Yeah, I understand." My voice was gruff. "You traded a supportive Boy Scout for a self-centered jerk."

"No! I got you. If you died, your ghost would still be trying to make me laugh. Holt, I didn't realize this until we started dating, but I only ever *liked* Jeremy. I *love* you."

My legs did buckle, and I took a very sudden seat on the floor.

Brittany sat next to me. "You had to know I love you. I moved to Seattle after only knowing you for a couple of months. I never told you because I didn't want to freak you out."

"But"—an image came to mind of Thanksgiving with Darren watching football on my couch—"this isn't all in my head. I asked you to join my family for Christmas months ago. You never even brought up Thanksgiving with your family."

"Oh…" Brittany tucked an invisible strand of hair behind her ear. "I'm sorry. It's just…Mom didn't meet you under the best circumstances and can't understand why I left Oregon to be near you. Then me not being home for Christmas was just one more betrayal." She shook her head. "I thought if it was just me for Thanksgiving, I could do some damage control."

"Okay." I was aware Mrs. Asato wasn't my biggest fan. Still, I wasn't thrilled with the confirmation. "Why didn't you tell me that?"

Britt's cheeks were pink. "I hate that my mom doesn't get you. I was too embarrassed, and I didn't realize how it looked."

Running a hand through my hair, I said, "But when you moved to Seattle, you said you needed a fresh start. You told me you wanted to leave Amelia's Haven. Wasn't I just a good excuse?"

Brittany almost rolled her eyes. "I did want to leave Amelia's Haven. Before we met, I was thinking Arizona."

"*Arizona!*" I sat up. "No one lives in *Arizona*. I have work conferences there. People don't live there."

She swatted my shoulder. "Don't badmouth Arizona. You have a bad thing to say about everywhere. I don't want to hear it about Arizona."

"Whatever," I said.

I shifted until my back was against the wall and my shoulder was touching Britt's. We sat in silence while I tried to process everything she'd said.

"Hold on." I turned to face her. "Just to be super-duper clear, you love me?"

"Yes." Britt sighed out the word like she was exasperated.

"You love me and I love you?"

Britt nodded.

I grinned so wide, my mouth hurt. "Then let's stop fighting and kiss already."

"Deal," Britt said.

A couple of kisses later, there was a knock on the door.

"Who is it?" Britt called—a little breathless.

Juniper barged in without an invitation. "Oh," she said and even had the decency to blush.

"Did you need something?" I asked, trying to stand up, only to discover my hands were tangled up in Britt's hair.

"Umm..." Juniper's doe eyes were huge.

"Juniper!"

"Oh, yeah. Mom said it's, uhh…time to build snowmen."

I groaned and rested my head on Britt's shoulder as she started laughing.

Of course it was time to build snowmen. Silly I'd expected anything else. If I wanted to kiss my girlfriend, Mom would need to add it to the schedule.

CHAPTER 13

"**N**ice trick, by the way," Juniper said as we walked downstairs.

"Right," I said, my mind still on the conversation with Britt.

Apparently Britt recovers from life-changing events faster than me, because she asked, "What did you do?"

"Umm..." I shrugged. "No idea."

Brittany and Juniper shared a look that was something like *He's not kidding*.

"My dear, kind brother, wise influence that he is, stole my stocking and wrote 'The Best' on Casey's stocking."

Huh?

"No, I didn't."

Juniper tapped a manicured finger to her lips. "Denial really doesn't look good on you."

I frowned. What I remembered was writing on Juniper's stocking. But that was right before my impromptu nap...Had I done something else?

"You got Holt's thinking face," Brittany said.

"Was he telling the truth?" Juniper stage-whispered.

Realizing I still had the marker in my pocket, I tossed it to Juniper. "Here," I said. "I wrote on your stocking, but—for obvious reasons—I'd never write 'The Best' on Casey's stocking. She's already overconfident."

"Then why did you steal mine?"

"Seriously?" (I sounded like a teenager.) "I have no idea who took your stocking."

We'd just reached the ground-floor landing when Britt said, "Did you mean to write 'The Best' on Juniper's stocking? You must've gotten hers confused with Casey's." Only the sparkling in her eyes gave away that she was kidding.

All the *I love yous* had left me warm and gooey inside, because instead of being annoyed, I grinned and backed Brittany against the wall. "You have the only stocking I'd write 'The Best' on."

"Oh yeah?" Brittany said—looking the most beautiful I'd ever seen her.

Before Britt could swoon or we could kiss, Juniper had my arm and was dragging me to the living room all while saying stuff like *Who are you?* and *What happened to my brother?*

Juniper didn't let go until I was in front of the mantel. "See?"

My sister was right. Her stocking had vanished, and in blue paint under Casey's name was the title, THE BEST.

"Well?" Juniper asked.

"Come on," I said. "I didn't do this. I wrote on your stocking, then had a chair nap with Harper, then I saw you in the kitchen, then I was with Mom and Dad, before Brittany and I..." I trailed off, too busy grinning. "Anyway, I had neither the time nor the mental energy to pull off a stocking heist."

"What did you write?" Brittany asked, having followed us into the living room.

"Yes!" Juniper said, like she'd only just now wondered that.

I sent Britt a warning look. If she kept stirring the pot, there'd be an all-out war by Christmas.

"Holt," Juniper and Brittany said in unison.

If someone had stolen Juniper's stocking to spare her feelings, the cat was still getting out of the bag. "'The Brat,'" I said, not quite making eye contact. "I wrote 'The Brat' on your stocking."

Brittany burst out laughing right as Juniper hit me with a couch cushion. I was wrestling the pillow away from Juniper when Mom's voice made us all freeze.

"None of you are ready for snowmen?" Mom let out an impatient breath. "Juniper, you had one job. Holt, you're a grown man. Why is this so difficult?"

Mom left, and from the sounds from outside, everyone else was on schedule. After a shocked silence, Juniper and I behaved like two mature adults and began giggling—well, I don't giggle, but you get the picture.

"Come on, you two," Britt said, leading the way to the foyer so we could get dressed in our snow gear. Britt wasn't laughing, but her face wasn't unnaturally calm, so she was probably okay.

When we were all bundled up, Juniper was the first out the door, with Brittany right behind her. "Hey," I said, grabbing Britt's arm. "I love you."

Britt's eyes sparkled. "I love you, too."

We stole a quick kiss before marching outside to build snowmen.

Here's the deal. To be able to work with snow, you need the proper snow at the right temperature. Ideally it's just above freezing, making the snow easy to pack, and then you get a good freeze after you're done to leave a slightly more permanent creation.

These weren't ideal temperatures. It was too cold for the snow to pack together. But Mom had scheduled building snowmen. She'd packed long carrots and colorful scarves. Snowmen were getting built.

Harper and Baxter bailed early to play in the snow. Then Juniper and Britt got out of the construction project by playing with the kids. Which left me, Mom, Dad, Casey, Nigel, and Jude struggling to pack snow together.

Oh yeah. And you know how I'm an engineer? That somehow gave my family the impression I'd be able to find solutions for inferior building materials.

After over a half hour of work, all the six of us had managed was one short and kind of dumpy snowman.

"Doggy!" Harper cried as the white Snow Beast suddenly emerged from the snow.

"Are we sure that's a dog?" Casey asked.

"Yeah," I said. "But unlike Chouzie, this one's not on social media."

"He should be," Juniper said.

The kids began chasing the Snow Beast. Twice they came dangerously close to toppling our only snowman, but somehow Jude always kept our frozen friend standing.

A whistle cut through the air, followed by a man's voice saying, "Shaka, come."

For a moment I couldn't spot the intruder in the midst of all the snow and trees. When I saw him, I instinctively reached for Britt. The man's features were hard to see, camouflaged in white snow gear. What was unmistakable were the two ice axes slung over his shoulder.

Was I about to meet my ax murderer?

The Snow Beast had gone obediently to its owner, but Harper and Baxter had followed. Then Mom started up a conversation with Mr. Ice Ax—like a man armed with two ice axes wasn't at all suspicious.

"Is there a way to tell if he's the killer?" Juniper whispered in my ear.

I shook my head.

Did Juniper really expect I'd have a sensational way to unmask a murderer? Saying something like *You gave yourself away with your left boot print* is for the bygone world of Sherlock Holmes, not for the current world of Holt Jacobs.

Mom was saying, "...a shame what happened last night."

My eyes locked with Juniper's. Was Mom the newest sleuth?

The man stared down at the snow as he said, "Yeah, Zeke tried to be a good guy."

"Who's Zeke?" I whispered to Juniper.

She shook her head. "The person you found last night."

Right. I knew that.

Mom's face had softened. The man probably thought she was being sympathetic, but I knew she was a lion ready to pounce. "Had you known Zeke long?"

Mr. Ice Ax kicked at a clump of snow. "I don't know. Sort of, I guess." He kicked at another clump of snow. "However long that youth camp's been coming here. That first year the power went out all along the road. We've got a backup generator and woodburning stoves, so they all stayed with us until the power was fixed. Zeke was really helpful with all that."

We've? He'd said *We've*. I probably should have put it together sooner, but that guy with the Snow Beast had to be with the Woman with the Snow Beast. I'd seen her driving the black truck, but was that their only vehicle? Had he been the man in the grocery store? And what was with the ice axes? Would Mom find a way to ask?

I must've leaned forward or made some sort of threatening movement, because suddenly the Snow Beast was charging at me. The dog was so fast, I didn't have time to react. But right before he crashed into me, the Snow Beast stopped, sat, and stared up at my face with his tail wagging.

"He thinks you'll play catch," Mr. Ice Ax said, striding over.

"Right," I said, looking from the owner to the dog. The animal was still waiting, tail thwapping against the snow, with some sort of doggy smile. Opening up my gloved hands, I said to the dog, "I don't have anything."

His tail gave a hard thump, but before he could burst into puppy tears, Baxter and Harper toppled over him and they all began playing again.

I let out a deep breath and felt my shoulders relax.

"Sorry about that," Mr. Ice Ax said. "Shaka's just friendly. He doesn't realize how scary he can come across."

I nodded. I wanted to say *I wasn't scared*. But when everyone knows you're lying, what's the point?

"It's fine," I said just as Juniper asked, "What's with the ice axes?"

I stared at Juniper. She's usually more subtle.

But since Juniper was asking, the guy didn't mind. "These?" he asked, swinging one casually in a way that had me taking a huge step back. "I do ice climbing tours."

I fought the urge to take another step back. This man was so comfortable using ice axes that he even led tours?

Mom was ready for this revelation. She said, "I somehow missed your tours when I was planning our trip."

Yikes. Mom wasn't kidding. She literally would have signed us all up for an ice ax hike. I'd only been saved from this fate because of his company's insufficient marketing.

The guy's face brightened. "Well, if you're ever back in the area, be sure to look us up." He bit off a glove with his teeth, pulled out his wallet, and handed Mom a business card.

"Thank you," she said. "Do a lot of people here use ice axes?"

The guy shrugged, surprisingly unsuspicious about this line of questioning. "Some. Here in Montana, the mountains offer so many outdoor options, you can really pick your poison."

"Has the youth group ever done one of your tours?" Brittany asked, deciding to join the questioning.

Mr. Ice Ax's eyes lit up. He was even more excited to have another person talking about his business. Like, he was so excited, he was an unlikely suspect. A man who's just used an ice ax as a murder weapon would probably feel self-conscious about advertising his ice climbing tours.

"Never officially," Mr. Ice Ax said, his eyes lingering on Britt a little longer than necessary. "Zeke was actually into it. He found out about my job, and we've gone out on a few climbs."

"Had you planned to go out this year?" I asked, finally getting a chance to ask a question.

"Yes." Something dimmed in his eyes. "It's stupid now, but Zeke accidentally took one of my ice axes home. It got mixed up with his supplies last year, and he was excited to be able to return it."

That explained why there was an ice ax on the scene and cleared up once and for all that the killer hadn't brought it.

At some point, while I was thinking things through, the man left. During that little interrogation, Jude, Nigel, Casey, and Dad had managed to build a second dumpy snowman.

Catching Jude's smirk as I evaluated their accomplishment, I accidentally smirked back. Weird. Had I just shared an inside joke with my silent brother-in-law?

"Good work, everyone," Mom said, admiring the snowmen. "Now let's get a few photos and head in for a quick bowl of chili. We need to be on the road in time for the Christmas Eve service."

There was a bit of a traffic jam as all ten of us tried to take off our snow gear in the entryway. I nearly elbowed Nigel in the face, but that was after Juniper stepped on my foot.

"Ankle Hold!" Harper was suddenly in front of me. "Help." She held her mittened hands up at me like they were puppy paws. Without thinking, I knelt down right into a puddle of melting snow. I clenched my jaw but didn't give any other sign of my mistake.

"Ankle Hold?" Harper was waiting.

Right.

I tried to be gentle as I removed the mittens. But they were so tight, it was difficult to remove them. It was no surprise Harper had been trapped.

Once the task was completed, Harper began struggling with all the Velcro on her jacket before getting at the zipper. That's when I noticed it. Her little hands were streaked with different colors of paint.

Paint? Like Casey's stocking.

"Harper," I asked—with everyone still in the entryway. "Who helped you paint?"

"Grandpa," Harper said, with her zipper halfway down.

Juniper gasped at Harper's testimony, and we both looked to where Dad was standing.

"You think Casey's *The Best*?" I asked.

"That's favoritism," Juniper said.

"What's going on?" Casey asked.

Dad held up his hands. "Settle down."

It was easy enough for me to be silent, but Juniper was actually quivering from keeping her mouth shut.

All eyes were on Dad, and he shifted uncomfortably with all the attention. "Juniper wrote on Holt's stocking. Holt wrote on Juniper's. Casey was the only one who didn't get involved with sibling rivalries." He winked at Casey. *"The Best."*

I let out a low whistle. "*The Brat*, *The Butt*, and *The Best*?"

"Sounds about right," Nigel said, kissing Casey.

"Hey!" Juniper said with only one boot on. "It still sounds like favoritism."

Dad frowned, but his eyes were twinkling. "I don't think so. The two of you were leaving Casey out, and I included her."

"But you wrote something nice," I pointed out.

Dad shrugged.

"And why did you steal my stocking?" Juniper asked.

"What?" Dad looked from Juniper to me. "I didn't touch your stocking."

"Then why's it missing?" Juniper asked.

There was a long silence; then all of us trooped into the living room to check. Juniper's stocking was still missing.

"Dad?" I asked.

His face was a little pale. "I don't know what happened. I swear."

"Okayyy," Juniper said. "Then where is it?"

No one spoke up.

"Who took it?" Jude asked in his quiet yet commanding voice.

Another silence followed. Everyone eyed each other with suspicion, and even Mom remained strangely silent.

Then came Harper's shy voice. "I 'ecorated Aunt Juniper's stocking like Ankle Hold did."

Casey was immediately at her daughter's side. "Sweetie, how were you able to reach it?"

Harper raised her chin—she was handling all the attention better than Dad had. "Baxter moved a chair and got it down for me, but then he left and I couldn't put it back."

"Can we go get it?" Casey asked.

We all waited as Casey and Harper went upstairs. After the glitter glue mess Harper had made on her own stocking, I couldn't imagine what she'd done to Juniper's.

Jude was waiting by the door and was the first person to see it. His face broke into a rare smile that lasted half a second.

Juniper rushed to his side and cried, "Oh, I love it!"

The stocking got turned toward the rest of the room. This time Harper's handiwork was rather minimal. Her only addition to Juniper's stocking was a bejeweled crown sticker, which she'd put on the top corner by Juniper's name.

"Well, sis," I said as Juniper rehung her stocking, "you really are a brat."

"She's a princess," Harper said, giving a twirl.

"That's right, Holt," Juniper said. "I'm not a brat. I'm a princess."

"Can't you be both?"

Before Juniper could reply, Mom cut in. "We really need to eat fast to make it to the church on time for the singing."

Singing?

Brittany's brain followed a similar track. "Do you sing?" she whispered as the room emptied.

I shrugged. "I *can* sing."

"So if I brought you to a karaoke bar, you'd—"

"I'd sit in the back drinking beer, mocking the performers, and asking when we could leave."

Britt tilted her head. "I think you'd sing for me." She flashed an almost wicked smile before following the group to the dining room.

Problem was, Britt was right. I'd tattoo her name on my forehead if she asked me to.

CHAPTER 14

I was the last person to get a bowl of chili. Casey's family was already upstairs getting dressed before I sat down. Even eating quickly, I was still behind schedule.

Then I ran into even more trouble when I tried to get dressed. Changing into black slacks and a crimson button-up proved impossible in my little pantry bedroom. The one time I attempted to take off my pants, Mom barged in without knocking because she was having a ziplock emergency.

In the end, I had to wait for an opening in the downstairs bathroom to get a chance to change and freshen up.

When I left the bathroom, the whole house was dark except for the Christmas lights and a lamp by the entryway. Dad stood waiting in the foyer. "Ready?" he asked.

I nodded and quickly put on my boots and coat.

"Casey's car left since they were all ready and your mom was worried about being late," Dad said.

As we walked to the SUV, Dad gestured toward the shotgun side of the vehicle. "You can sit up front."

It wasn't until I was in the SUV that I saw the problem. Britt wasn't there. There were only two people in the back seats, and they were Juniper and Jude snuggled up together.

Had my family forgotten her?

"Where's Britt?" I asked.

At first no one answered. Finally Dad said, "She was ready and waiting by the door, so Mom had her ride in Casey's car."

What?! Not only was I being denied Britt's company, but now she was trapped in a vehicle with my mother. Britt could hold her own, but sooner or later everyone cracks under Mom's interrogation.

"How long?" I asked.

"*How long?*" Juniper repeated, half giggling.

I twisted in my seat to glare at her. "How long of a drive is it?"

"Mom said it's over an hour away."

Over an hour? Britt was stuck with Mom for over an hour?

I tried calling Britt's phone as Dad began to drive. It didn't even ring before I was sent to her voicemail. "Come on," I muttered. Then I texted: *Are you okay? Call me.*

The message had a spinning wheel next to it as it tried to send.

"I don't want to say you're codependent," Juniper said in a singsongy voice, "but you're panicking about not seeing your girl-friend for an hour."

When I turned to face her, she was still wrapped securely in Jude's arms. "And I don't want to say you're bad company, but Brittany smells a lot nicer than you."

Juniper gave a fake gasp, like I'd shocked her, but otherwise remained silent.

The drive should have been peaceful. The roads were good, and it was a clear night with the moon shining across the snow. I might have even enjoyed myself if Brittany were in the car. As it was, I kept checking my phone. The text I'd written was still trying to send.

At one point I complained about how bad reception was in the mountains, and even Juniper thought it best to ignore me.

Was Mom grilling Britt? What kind of dirt was she after?

We drove through the Christmas town and then began climbing up another mountain road. I checked the time but didn't remember when we'd left the lodge. Crossing my arms, I asked, "Why is the church beyond nowhere?"

That was a question my baby sister decided to answer. "It has the most amazing views. I've seen some wedding photos that were taken there, and they're absolutely stunning."

I sighed and slumped in my seat. *Cool story, bro. Except it's pitch dark, so what's the point?*

"It's a famous structure," Dad said. "Your mom found it on a list of top places to see in Montana."

Given the dark road, Dad couldn't really see the unimpressed glare I sent him.

"They built an extension thirty years ago," Juniper said—apparently she'd read the same article Mom had. "But most of the original structure is still standing."

"It's probably not built to code," I grumbled, and everyone was surprised when Jude half snorted.

Finally the parking lot with its streetlights became visible before the actual building came into view. It looked how you'd expect. Old and wooden, with large windows to show off the mountain views in daylight but showed off everything inside the building at night.

Before anyone could comment, my phone lit up with Brittany calling me.

"Did you survive?" I asked.

"What? Oh." Britt's light laugh filled the line. "Yes, it was fine. Nothing to get worked up about."

"Nothing to get worked up about?" My voice was louder than necessary. "Brittany, it's my mom. Give her five minutes in a room with someone and she could steal their identity."

"If I start getting suspicious credit card alerts, I'll let you know."

"Britt"—I lowered my voice, though everyone in the SUV could definitely still hear me—"did Mom pressure you into saying anything?"

"What?" Britt sounded confused. "We just talked about random things."

"Such as?" Call me overly suspicious, but there was no way Mom *accidentally* spent an hour alone with my girlfriend. (Yes, technically Casey's whole family was in the Suburban, but right now they didn't count.)

"I don't know...I asked her about Australia and whether she's seen many kangaroos. She said she's seen plenty of kangaroos and invited me to visit."

Visit Australia?

Australia? No way. Mom's big ploy for getting Britt by herself was to invite her to Australia?

Apparently I'd tuned out reality because Juniper was saying, "Holt," and tugging at my arm.

I moved out of Juniper's reach before returning to my phone call. Who knows what else Britt might have said.

"Sorry about that. I kind of spaced out."

But her side of the call was muffled, like she was talking to someone else.

When she returned to the line, she sounded distracted. "Are you almost here?"

"Uh, yeah. Dad's trying to find a parking spot."

"Good," she said. "When you enter the sanctuary, our seats are to the right and halfway down." Then either the call dropped or Brittany hung up without saying goodbye.

Right as Dad found a spot, a police car flashed its lights and took the space. In the end Dad settled for the overflow field, and we had to tromp through packed-down snow to get to the pavement. We were almost to the parked cop car when an officer appeared from the opposite direction leading a handcuffed Mr. Ice Ax.

"Holt, look!" Juniper whispered.

"Uh-huh," I said. It appeared Mr. Ice Ax was being arrested for murder, yet I was nagged by doubt.

Had the police caught the *real* killer?

CHAPTER 15

Mr. Ice Ax's arrest should have been a relief. Maybe it would've been, if I thought he was actually the killer.

What evidence did the police have?

When we entered the church, the large foyer was almost empty of people, while the muffled sounds of singing came through the open double doors.

The Woman with the Snow Beast was in the lobby, frowning down at her phone. In the spirit of Christmas, I skipped hanging up my coat to talk to her. "You know the police came and...?" I trailed off. It's awkward to comment on the arrest of someone's spouse.

"Yes." She seemed both embarrassed and relieved to see me. "I was trying to find a lawyer. But would anyone be working on Christmas Eve?"

No one good *is working on Christmas Eve* is what I thought—but I managed to keep that on the inside. I attempted to be reassuring. "I'm sure you'll find someone."

"He didn't do this," she said.

"Of course he didn't."

What I said wasn't a total lie. Right now there was no way of knowing whether Mr. Ice Ax was guilty. And my gut was telling me he wasn't the killer.

"But"—it was probably rude to ask; still, the possible dog prints by the wreck were suspicious—"wasn't your dog at the crime scene today?"

"Shaka? How did you know?"

I shrugged. "We had to wait as they towed away the car."

The woman frowned. "Is that why they made the arrest?"

"I—"

Before I could speak a full sentence, the Woman with the Snow Beast was interrupting. "Because if that's the case, this is all a big misunderstanding. I had Shaka in the truck bed and slowed down to get a better look at the crash. He must've thought we were stopping, because he jumped out and ran around."

"You didn't walk around the crime scene?"

She pressed her lips together, running low on patience. "No way."

Huh. It made sense. And would explain why the dog prints were there. Plus, having your dog run around a crime scene wouldn't be a smart move as a murderer.

"But"—I had to ask—"why did you slow down?"

"Umm." Heat flooded the woman's face. "I wanted to know if some of my husband's personal property was in the car."

"The ice ax," I said.

Her mouth hung open—both of us were surprised I'd just said that.

"Is everything all right?" My dad's quiet voice broke through. He'd joined us, with Juniper and Jude right behind him.

"Well…" It wasn't really my business to share the Woman with the Snow Beast's personal problems. Sure, Dad had seen Mr. Ice Ax's arrest, but I couldn't exactly tell him about the evidence in front of the suspect's wife. "Um, this is my father, my little sister, and her husband."

She gave a half smile. "Nice to meet you." Ingrained politeness momentarily made her forget her husband's arrest.

Before anything else could be said, Brittany appeared from the sanctuary. "There you are. Your mom was worried you got lost. It's starting."

Of course it was. The singing could be heard from the parking lot.

Before I could point this out, the Woman with the Snow Beast's face scrunched up as she looked from me to Brittany. "Where's your daughter?"

Britt's eyes widened. "Our what?"

I winced. Why hadn't I seen this coming?

But really, Harper wouldn't look like a child I'd have with Brittany—not that I'd thought about what our children might look like. Still, I'd assume our kids would have Brittany's black hair and brown eyes, instead of my blond hair and green eyes. Which was fine with me. If I had kids, they might as well resemble the most beautiful woman in the world.

"Whose daughter?" Juniper asked, always ready to be in the middle of things.

"Holt?" Dad asked. Apparently I was frozen in place.

"Right, uh"—no need to be ashamed, just a simple misunderstanding—"that was actually my niece you saw me with this morning. She's inside with her parents."

"I see," the woman said. But from the look on her face, she was more confused than before.

There was a long pause during which both Britt and I made a point of *not* looking at each other. For once my brother-in-law broke the silence. "Let me walk you to your car," Jude offered. *Has the Christmas spirit bitten everyone?* "Do you know where the police station is?"

"Um, yes. Thank you." The Woman with the Snow Beast shot one more questioning glance in my direction before allowing Jude to walk her outside.

Britt waited until after they'd exited to ask, "She said Harper was your daughter this morning?"

I nodded.

"You didn't correct her?" Juniper asked. "Why didn't you correct her?"

I shrugged.

"Normal people would clear that up."

Thankfully, we entered the sanctuary, and hundreds of voices singing "Joy to the World" drowned out my sister.

It was impossible to concentrate during the Christmas service. I didn't even notice when Jude returned. He just suddenly appeared beside Juniper. Britt could tell I was off and squeezed my hand a couple of times, but I behaved appropriately given the setting—I just didn't hear a word.

Was Mr. Ice Ax really the killer?

His wife's black truck had driven past the accident during the time of the murder.

When I'd spoken to the Woman with the Snow Beast, she said she'd been on the road. Had her husband been with her? If so, could he have pulled over, claimed he was going to check out the accident, and calmly murdered someone with his own ax before returning to the truck and driving away? And if that were true, wouldn't his wife figure that out?

Behind me I could hear snickers and general unrest. When I glanced back, I found the group of teens filling the rows by the exit. For a moment my eyes caught Wyatt's, and my brain jolted with a realization.

How had I been so stupid?

When I'd questioned Wyatt and he said he'd walked from the crash to their cabin, I never asked him *how many* vehicles drove past.

Wyatt said when he woke up, Zeke was slumped over the steering wheel, so Zeke had to have been alive then. But had Wyatt been unconscious when the black truck drove past?

I hadn't noticed the wreck. It was Britt who'd spotted it. What if Mr. Ice Ax or his wife had driven by without noticing the crash?

I needed to ask Wyatt how many cars had driven past him.

I glanced down at the program, trying to figure out which talking part we were at—it would have helped if I'd remembered which songs we'd already sung.

Running a hand through my hair, I tried to be patient. The murder had happened last night, and with all the family stuff going on, it was understandable I hadn't figured out the driver of the silver sedan. But I needed to know who all the suspects were.

Who knows. Maybe Mr. Ice Ax drove the silver sedan while his wife used the black truck.

Was that what the police had figured out? Both vehicles belonged to the same house? Otherwise what evidence could they have?

Maybe they'd realized the ax Zeke was returning belonged to Mr. Ice Ax. Was that enough for an arrest?

Britt placed a hand on my knee and gave me a *hold still* look. I'd probably been fidgeting. Letting out a breath, I did my best to sit and act like I was paying attention. I did a fine job, yet I couldn't stop myself from glancing back at Wyatt from time to time.

I needed to talk to him.

Finally we were singing one last carol and getting dismissed.

I tried to bolt, but I may as well have been stuck in the back of an airplane with everyone in front of me crowding the aisle, trying to get their bags from the overhead bins. We were in the middle of a crowded pew, and everyone was chatting, annoyingly full of holiday cheer.

"Are you okay?" Brittany whispered.

I nodded, since the middle of a crowded church wasn't the place to start spouting murder theories.

"You're flushed," she said.

I shrugged. "I just need to get out."

Britt took a moment to analyze my face before plastering on a fake smile and saying, "Excuse us," to half a million people, before successfully dragging me out of the sanctuary. The foyer wasn't much better. It was also packed with people, who were filling small plates with cookies and munching on them in little groups.

"What's going on?" Juniper asked, catching up with us.

Brittany began to answer as I caught a flash of red hair in the distance. I left them without a word of explanation. I couldn't lose track of Wyatt.

But somehow Wyatt vanished in the crowd. Did he know I was following him? Or maybe he'd just left. The men's room was right next to the exit, and I checked in there before zipping up my winter coat and heading outside.

What was Wyatt up to? If I were him, I'd be heaping a plate full of cookies, not wandering around a dark parking lot—assuming he'd gone outside.

I did my best to patrol the rows of parked cars. A few people had started trickling to their vehicles, but almost everyone was inside chatting. While it would have been easy for Wyatt to hide behind a van, as far as I could tell, he wasn't in the parking lot.

Next I circled the outside of the church. But there were no obvious signs of him there. I even went down an outdoor staircase and tried a door that led to the church's basement, but the door wouldn't budge.

On my way back to the main entrance, I froze. A silver sedan was parked right in front of me. I shivered, suddenly noticing the eerie December night.

Who knows how many silver sedans were driving around Montana. And even if this was the same silver sedan from the gas station footage, that didn't mean the driver was the killer. Maybe the killer was Mr. Ice Ax and the silver sedan was his. If so, he was already in police custody.

Whatever the reality, I hurried back inside to the safety of light and other people.

Starting with the foyer, I made a more careful search for Wyatt. There were slightly fewer people around, and still Wyatt was missing. Next I tried the sanctuary. Inside was a group of Wyatt's friends, but again the redhead was missing. I ended my hunt by looking once more in the bathroom.

The stalls were empty.

I don't know what it was about staring at my reflection in the bathroom mirror, but I realized a new problem—when I'd checked the entire church, I hadn't spotted a single family member.

They wouldn't...They couldn't have forgotten me on Christmas Eve.

Right?

Quickly exiting the bathroom, I checked the church. My family wasn't there. Bolting outside, I jogged through the parking lot to the overflow area where Dad had parked.

The SUV was missing.

Next I walked row by row, checking every vehicle, trying to find Casey's Suburban. As I looked, I tried calling Brittany's phone and was sent straight to voicemail. Not good.

Then I tried calling every single family member. When that didn't work, I even tried calling my brothers-in-law, hoping one of them would have a better service provider. But nothing worked. It didn't matter that I had five bars of reception. None of my calls went through.

I'd been abandoned on Christmas Eve. So fun.

There'd probably been a mix-up, and each vehicle thought I was in the other one. If that was true, this wouldn't be discovered until after they'd driven the hour-plus back to the lodge. Then they'd have to drive another hour-plus just to get me, before an additional hour-plus drive to get back to the cabin.

This would be a long night.

At this point the parking lot was half-full. It was unlikely there'd still be people around in the two hours it took my family to get me.

Not loving any of my options, I decided *not freezing* was the best and headed into the church one more time.

The trays of cookies were definitely picked over, but I grabbed a plate and ended up with a decent spread. Problem was, the church now seemed to only have locals, and I was getting curious glances. Plus, my black slacks stuck out in a room full of jeans.

Since having a stranger try to make friendly small talk with me would be worse than getting abandoned, I did something kind of gross and brought my plate of cookies to the men's room, where I could eat in peace.

There were a few feet of extra space behind the bathroom door, where some brilliant genius had put a bench. Sitting down, I tried to enjoy my cookies. Not an easy task when I'd lost Wyatt, a silver sedan was parked out front, my family had ditched me, and I was hanging out in a bathroom hoping no one would come in to use the facilities.

I set my phone's stopwatch so I could have a rough estimate of how long before my family would get to the lodge.

If the thought of strangers talking to me hadn't left me with an itchy feeling down my spine, I'd be out in the lobby waiting to see who belonged to the silver sedan. And if my body was more used to the cold, I'd be watching from outside. As it was, I didn't want to risk hypothermia and frostbite.

My winter coat was zipped up all the way, and I was beginning to get nicely warm. I stretched my legs out across the bench, leaned against the wall, and waited for the hour to run out.

I was startled out of a doze by the door creaking open and the light switching off. Were they locking up the church? I blinked a few times—not that I could see anything in the darkness. How long had I been out?

I shouldn't stay inside after the church was locked up. That definitely felt wrong. But as I stood in the pitch-black room, my phone lit up with Juniper's name.

"Hey," I said, my voice a little gravelly.

"What's with all the missed calls? What was so important you had to call me, Dad, and Jude? I thought you'd be too busy hanging out with your girlfriend."

Before I could answer, there was the sound of a door opening, garbled words from lots of people, and then Britt's voice came through clearly. "Where's Holt?"

"Uh-oh," Juniper said.

In the distance Mom asked, "What is it?"

"We forgot Holt."

At this point Juniper must've covered the speaker because everything became too muffled to understand.

Then Britt was on the line. "Are you okay?" She managed to sound concerned and amused at the same time.

"I'm great," I said. "It's not like my family forgot me on Christmas Eve."

Mom must've asked how I was, since the next thing Brittany said was, "He's fine."

"I'm not fine!"

Britt ignored my comment, instead saying, "Juniper and I are heading out in her car. We'll be there as soon as we can."

"Okay," I said, knowing this was the only option.

"Sorry, babe," she said. "The kids were fading, so we all just piled back into Casey's Suburban. I had no idea people thought you were with us."

"Well," I said, trying to be slightly less grumpy, "as you said, I'm fine."

I think Brittany started laughing, but the phone began cutting out and then the line went dead.

Good news. My rescue party was only an hour away. Yippee.

After the call dropped, I remembered I was standing in a pitch-black bathroom. I left once I found the door handle. The foyer was completely dark except for a couple of safety lights and the glow through the windows from the streetlights in the parking lot.

Great.

I was now locked inside a deserted church. Getting out would be easy. The doors were the push kind, and it didn't look like there was any sort of alarm system. But I was left with a sort of moral dilemma. Was it trespassing to accidentally stay in a church after it had been locked up? And if it technically *wasn't* trespassing, was it still morally wrong?

Before I could decide, my phone began vibrating, and this time it was Mom.

"I can't believe this happened," she said before I said a word. "We were supposed to all be drinking eggnog and eating gingerbread right now while talking about what we're thankful for."

My grip on the phone tightened. I didn't like where this was headed.

"How hard is it for you to get into a vehicle?"

There it was.

Trying not to sound frustrated, I said, "It's not hard when people tell me it's time to go." I sighed. "Shouldn't your mom-senses tell you when I'm missing?"

"Oh!" That struck a nerve. "Well...I don't know exactly how to explain it, but my *mom-senses* have dulled since you started dating Brittany. I'm not exactly sure why, but the same thing happened when Casey and Juniper started dating their husbands."

An unexpected grin tugged at my lips. "Good for Britt."

Mom's answer was noncommittal. "She is something." There was a crash in the distance. Mom said, "I have to go. Love you." Then she hung up.

Another crash sounded.

I jumped.

Was that coming from the church?

I checked my phone, the call had ended. That sound had come from here. In this empty building.

I stood frozen, waiting for another noise. When it came, this time there was also a voice complaining, though the words were unintelligible.

But wherever the noise was, it wasn't coming from the foyer or the sanctuary.

Was it beneath my feet?

Was someone in the basement?

I walked around the inside of the church's perimeter but didn't find any doors leading downstairs. Could the only way down really be the set of stairs I'd found outside?

As I stood considering my options, I heard faint calls for help.

Maybe it was my lifeguard training kicking in, but my feet were propelling me outside before my mind could consider whether it was even a good idea. Rounding the corner to the stairs, I froze. The entire parking lot was empty except for the silver sedan.

Yikes.

Was I being paranoid? It didn't mean the driver was the killer.

Another shout had me heading for the stairs. This time the door was ajar, and it looked like it'd been forced. Peering inside, I found a hallway full of doors. It was a high-ceilinged basement—the type that probably had a basketball court.

The door closest to me had latch locks on the outside. A frustrated yell came from that room. Someone was definitely trapped inside. Looking around, I didn't see any signs of danger, so I entered the hallway and began undoing the latches.

I don't know who I was expecting to find when I flung the door open, but it sure wasn't Wyatt with his hands behind his back and tied to a pipe.

He rolled his eyes when he saw me. "Of course it's you."

What was that supposed to mean? And he could be a little more excited about getting rescued.

The room seemed to be an abandoned storage room, with nothing but a few paint cans inside. There wasn't a light switch, so the only light was what drifted in through the door and a basement window high up along the wall.

Checking the hallway one more time, I wedged a paint can in between the door before going to Wyatt.

When I got close, he began kicking at me. His first kick landed painfully on my shin, but I moved back before he could hit me again.

Reminding myself I was the mature adult, I held up my hands. "Relax. Let me untie you."

A little of Wyatt's anger disappeared, but it was replaced by fear. "Why?"

"Um"—*wasn't it obvious?*—"so we can get out of here."

For some reason that was the wrong thing to say. Wyatt resumed kicking even though I was beyond his reach. "I'm not going anywhere with you."

"Come on," I said, checking the door. "We don't have time for this. Let me free you."

Wyatt didn't calm down, so I tried a different tack. "Who did this?"

"You know!" Wyatt's voice was full of teenage contempt.

"No, I don't." I sighed when Wyatt's face remained tense. "Look, I was here with my family for the Christmas service. The only reason I'm still here is because they forgot me. I heard you calling and came to check."

Wyatt relaxed a little after my speech but remained skeptical. "Then why did you keep staring at me during church?"

"I wasn't staring!" I frowned. The teen had gotten to me again. I lowered my voice. "I wanted to ask you how many cars drove past when you walked to the cabin last night."

"Sure." Wyatt nodded slowly like he thought I was crazy.

"Can you tell me?" I said, moving slowly to get to where he was tied up. Wyatt stiffened when my hands touched his wrists, but he didn't start kicking.

"Um, I couldn't really see them. But it was two vehicles."

Two vehicles had passed? Mr. Ice Ax really could be the killer.

"A black truck and a silver car?" I asked.

"No." Wyatt craned his neck to look at me. "It was a silver car and a red car."

Red? The only red vehicle had been mine, and I'd driven past after the murder had been committed. That meant the killer really was the driver of the silver sedan.

"Who did this to you?" I asked again, fumbling with the final knots.

"I did." For a second The Chaperone stood in the doorway, momentarily framed with light. Then the door slammed shut and the locks clicked into place before I could get to the door.

"Come on!" I yelled, trying to yank open the door.

"It's too late," The Chaperone said through the door. "If you and Wyatt went to the police with what you know, they'd think I was some sort of murderer."

And you're not? Thankfully, I kept that thought on the inside.

"Sure you're not a killer," I said. Wyatt snorted, but maybe the sound didn't travel through the door.

"It's definitely him," Wyatt whispered. "I was outside hiding from you when he grabbed me and started rambling about how I'd figured it out. Then he forced me into the basement and tied me up."

I couldn't stop my groan. Wyatt hadn't even solved the murder, but The Chaperone was so paranoid he'd incorrectly assumed.

"This is all one big misunderstanding," I called. "Why not open the door and we can talk about it?"

"Nice try," The Chaperone said.

"All right. Let's talk through the door," I said, since all the TV shows say it's better if a kidnapper feels a connection to their hostages. "You're clearly a good person," I tried. "You volunteer your vacations to chaperone teenagers. When you drove by the accident, you must've pulled over to help"—*What was his name?*—"him."

"Mr. Zeke," Wyatt whispered.

"Yes. You were just trying to help Zeke, because that's the type of person you are."

There was scuffling on the other side of the door, so I knew he was still there, but The Chaperone didn't answer. Maybe I'd laid it on too thick. This was what I got for telling lies in a church on Christmas Eve.

Suddenly the door vibrated like The Chaperone had hit it. "I am a good person," he said. "I work really hard for everything I have, but Zeke never saw it that way."

"How did Zeke see it?" I asked, willing to talk about anything The Chaperone found appropriate.

"He thought I was tagging along on trips because I have a crush on Miss Stacy." He gave a sick laugh. "I'm an adult. I don't get crushes."

"Of course not," I said, because agreeing with the ax murderer seemed like the best option.

"He has a *huge* crush," Wyatt said—at least attempting to whisper. "He got super jealous when Mr. Zeke made Miss Stacy laugh."

I nodded. Jealousy made sense. And aside from the whole being trapped thing, I felt pretty good about sensing something was wrong with that guy. I'd been right. Inviting a vampire into your home or co-owning a timeshare with a creep were both bad ideas.

"Did Zeke take Stacy from you?" I asked, trying to sound like I understood what he was going through.

"This isn't about Stacy!" The Chaperone yelled so loudly it was a wonder the door didn't vibrate. "This is all about Zeke being a vain know-it-all who was actually an idiot." The Chaperone took a deep breath like he'd run out of air. "Like last year Zeke was going off on an ice climb." The Chaperone's voice was bitter. "When I tried to go, too, Zeke said I couldn't tag along like I was some little kid. I've been doing climbs like that for over a decade, but Mr. Perfect didn't care."

The Chaperone fell silent, but my gut said he'd tell me everything if I waited. In the quiet, there were sounds, almost like something was being dragged in the hallway.

"I even drove to the retreat in my car so Zeke wouldn't accuse me of trying to spend hours sitting next to Stacy." There came a sound that was almost a roar. "I shouldn't have been out there when he crashed, but one of the kids forgot a pillow, so I bought one at the store. On my way back, I saw him in the ditch." The Chaperone gave a hollow laugh. "But, when I pulled over to help, he was trying to use that stupid ice ax as a shovel to clear a path for his car." There was a thud in the hallway like something heavy had dropped. "I told him to get in my car and we'd go get help, but he was so sure he could solve the problem and just kept flailing that ice ax around like he knew how to use it."

The Chaperone went silent then. After waiting a few moments, I asked, "So you took it from him?"

"Yeah." His voice was more subdued. "I took it and showed him how to use it."

Eesh.

I glanced back at Wyatt to make sure he wasn't horribly traumatized. His face was a unique combination of bored and annoyed, so he was probably fine...for still being tied to a pipe.

There were more scuffling sounds, and then the smell of gasoline drifted through the air.

No, no, no. This man wasn't going to burn me alive.

"See, it's all one big misunderstanding," I said, hoping The Chaperone couldn't hear the panic in my voice. "What could Wyatt or I even tell the police? Come on, buddy, you're being paranoid."

The Chaperone was still moving around the hallway, but he didn't answer. At least I didn't smell any smoke.

"Look, I don't think we've been formally introduced," I said, trying to buy more time. "My name's Holt, and you already know Wyatt. Can you tell me your name?"

After a pause, he said, "It's William."

"Nice to meet you, William," I said.

William didn't acknowledge the greeting. Instead, he said, "Hey, Holt? Merry Christmas."

There was a strange almost flicking sound, and then the door to the outside slammed shut.

William The Chaperone was gone.

A second later there was smoke.

CHAPTER 16

For a moment I rested my head on the door and took a deep breath.

This couldn't be happening.

When I turned around to face Wyatt, I tried to grin. "Let's get you out of here."

Wyatt didn't fight me as I worked to untie the final knot. Plus, his teenage skepticism almost hid the fear in his eyes. "Pretty sure you're as trapped as I am."

I was tempted to ask Wyatt to tone down the snark, but I couldn't take away the kid's only coping mechanism. I also didn't point out that since I wasn't tied up, that made me less trapped by default.

Once Wyatt was free, I did what I should have done when I first heard him shouting—I called the police. Or, I *tried* to call the police, but I didn't have any service. The cement walls in the basement were blocking my signal.

"Do you have reception?" I asked Wyatt.

He shook his head. "I don't have my phone. Miss Stacy was afraid we'd text during church, so she made us leave them at the house."

Super.

Wyatt coughed. Then his tongue did a weird smacking thing. "Is it getting smoky?"

"Yup. Your thoughtful chaperone is trying to cook us."

"On Christmas Eve?"

I nodded.

"In a church?"

I nodded again.

"That's like...really bad."

"My thoughts exactly," I muttered, turning on my phone's flashlight to take better stock of the room.

There was a door I couldn't open with a fire burning just outside, a tiny window I couldn't reach, and a few cans of paint. My life was turning into that dumb riddle where you're trapped in a room with no openings and the only items inside are a mirror and a table.

Wyatt coughed again.

When I looked his way, he shrugged. "I have asthma."

Of course he did.

I had to get Wyatt out of here before the smoke got too bad.

Britt and Juniper would be arriving sometime soon, but even if they called 911 right away, who knew how long it would be before the firemen came. I had to work with what I had. Tonight that was paint cans.

I handed Wyatt my phone and had him shine it on the wall with the window.

"Stand back," I warned.

I took a paint can and hurled it at the window. It banged uselessly against the wall before hitting the floor. The lid busted off and half a gallon of tan paint oozed across the floor.

"Were you in the major leagues?"

Sure my aim had been off, but you try throwing an unevenly weighted cylinder at a small target twelve feet in the air. I glared at Wyatt before picking up another can.

My second attempt actually hit the window, leaving a crack snaking across the pane.

This can hadn't burst, so I threw it again. I heard the shattering of glass but couldn't see it happen due to my phone's light bouncing around the room as Wyatt had a coughing fit.

Ignoring my scratchy throat, I took the phone from Wyatt and shone it at the window. Lucky for me, the paint can had busted through the glass and was now somewhere in the parking lot.

Wyatt was wheezing beside me and I was starting to feel dizzy. He only wore a flannel shirt, so I unzipped my winter coat. "Put this on."

"Why?" Wyatt asked. "With the fire going, things should get pretty toasty."

I took a deep breath and managed to sound calm as I explained, "Your emergency exit is ready, but I don't want you getting cut by the glass on your way out."

"What?" Wyatt put on the coat but didn't zip it up. "I can't reach that window, and even if I could, I wouldn't fit."

I sighed. Saving someone's life shouldn't be so difficult.

"I'll give you a boost, and I'm sure you'll make it."

Actually, the engineer in me was like eighty-five percent sure he would fit, but even if Wyatt got stuck partway through, his head would still be outside breathing fresh air.

I stood right beneath the broken window, crunching over shards of broken glass—thankfully the wet paint was mostly puddled a couple of feet away.

"Come on," I said.

Finally Wyatt zipped up my jacket and joined me by the wall.

"Now what?"

"Uh...shoulder ride?" It came out as a question when I was going for confident.

"Sure thing, boss."

Wyatt tried to hand me the phone. I shook my head. "Keep it. When you get out of here, call 911."

This time Wyatt didn't argue. He put the phone in an inside pocket of my coat. Without the flashlight, the only light came from the street-lights outside the small window.

Needless to say, getting Wyatt onto my shoulders was an awkward business. The first attempt had Wyatt falling hard against the wall while I slid to the ground and ended up sprawled in glass shards and tan paint.

"Again," I wheezed—from smoke (not physical exertion).

Standing up, I tried to shake off the glass and wiped off the hand that was wet with paint on a dry section of my pants. The pain was easier to ignore than the fact I'd just ruined my clothes.

Wyatt and I reset. This time he made it successfully onto my shoulders.

"Now what?" Wyatt asked, still a few feet away from the window.

"Now stand on my shoulders."

Wyatt half laughed as he said, "Yeah."

My head was growing fuzzier, and the room was turning hazy with smoke. I couldn't keep this up much longer. "Come on," I said, moving my hands to create a step for Wyatt to stand on.

There was more fumbling, and Wyatt almost yanked out my hair in an effort not to fall, but he was finally standing on my shoulders.

"I can't reach," Wyatt said, then burst into another coughing fit—almost toppling the two of us. Good thing there was a wall to lean against.

"How far?" I asked.

"I don't know. A few inches?"

My brain was racing, my whole body now alerting me to smoke inhalation. I had to focus. Clearing my throat, I asked, "You know that cheerleader lift where the guy holds the girl's foot in his fully extended arms?"

"You were a cheerleader?"

Seriously, Wyatt? Not the time.

"No. I was never a cheerleader. But now seems like a good time to give it a try."

We were partway through this transition—one of Wyatt's feet was half raised in my hands—when my foot began to lose traction in paint that had slowly pooled toward me.

"Wyatt!" I called, the only warning I could think of.

"Almost there."

Right when I was about to drop the both of us, the weight above me vanished.

I still fell and hit my ribs badly as I landed in more glass and paint.

Groaning, I rolled over to look up. But the light was almost completely gone. As far as I could tell, Wyatt was wedged partway through the window, but he wasn't exactly fitting.

"Come on," I muttered. Ignoring my throbbing ribs, I got to my feet and repositioned myself. Getting Wyatt's dangling feet in my hands, I gave him a shove with all I had left, and he was able to wriggle through.

I sank, gasping, to the floor, my lungs burning from smoke and pain.

Wyatt's head popped in through the window. "What about you?"

At first I was panting too hard to answer, but when I could speak, I grinned and said, "I'm stuck down here. Even if I could reach the window, there's no way my shoulders could make it through."

"But...but..."

"Wyatt, I'll be fine. Call for help and hide until you see the police."

"No! You can't stay here."

My mind was swirling, but I had to stay strong. "Please"—my voice cracked either from smoke or emotion—"tell the police what happened."

"Okay," Wyatt said, only he didn't sound like some arrogant teen. He sounded like a scared little kid.

"Thank you," I said. Our eyes locked for a moment, and then Wyatt was gone.

I almost passed out right then, but I struggled to stay conscious. Mom would kill me if I died on Christmas Eve.

Trying to remember proper fire protocols, I removed my pants and stuffed them under the crack by the door. That side of the room was growing very hot, and my eyes burned as I shoved my pants into place.

The only other things I could think of were staying low to the ground and having a damp cloth over my face. There weren't any sinks nearby, but I took off my button-up and—once I found a section that wasn't soaked with paint—began to breathe through it. Then I lay down by the wall with the window. At this point, what harm were a few more glass shards and some more paint?

My head rested in a puddle of paint, but I was too exhausted to care. I was a total mess, covered in paint and glass, wearing nothing but boxers, socks, and shoes.

I closed my eyes to block out the smoke and tried to remember all the yoga stuff I'd learned when Juniper made me go. I lay more or less in corpse pose. All that was left was to relax and remain calm.

Breathe in. Breathe out. Breathe in.

What if The Chaperone was in the parking lot and caught Wyatt?

Breathe in. Breathe—

And where was Britt? She was supposed to pick me up soon. Was she safe?

Breathe in. Breathe out. Breathe in. Breathe out.

Problem was it was becoming harder and harder to focus on anything...even my breathing. My brain was tingling, and there was a rushing in my ears. Momentarily forgetting where I was, I opened my eyes only to close them immediately as the smoke stung them.

Breathe. Breathe. Breathe.

All I could hear was the crackling fire. All I could feel was its heat.

Breathe. Come on. Breathe.

A darkness descended on me. Something way different from falling asleep. I tried to fight it, but it had ahold of me and was pulling me down. Soon the sounds of the fire faded away.

CHAPTER 17

S omewhere far away were voices.

Voices, then blackness.

Then voices again, followed by more blackness.

And my name. Someone was saying my name over and over again. Someone so insistent, it must've been Mom.

No. It wasn't time to wake up.

"Holt!" I was being shaken, and the voice wasn't Mom's.

It was Britt. That voice could only belong to Brittany. I wanted to say her name, but my body was ignoring my brain's signals.

I managed to crack an eye open, and I found Britt hovering over me. We were in an ambulance, and an oxygen mask covered my mouth and nose.

She looked so worried. I had to do something. I fought to stay conscious as I tried to take the mask off, my hand trembling.

"Don't worry, Holt," Britt said, trying to keep me from removing the mask. "You're safe."

I met her eyes, and whatever she saw there was enough for her to let me remove the mask. "Britt," I rasped in a voice that wasn't mine.

"Yes?"

"The harp music in heaven isn't so bad."

"Holt!" Then Brittany started laugh-crying.

I did my best to grin and didn't fight it when she put the mask back on.

After this the details get kind of fuzzy. I slipped into a half-conscious reality where I could speak when spoken to but was good for little else.

Once we got to the hospital, a new round of people began fussing over me. This detail may have been a hallucination, but I'm pretty sure my main nurse was wearing elf scrubs, with bells that jingled when she moved. Even that wasn't enough to catch my attention.

It was Mom's voice that snapped me out of my daze. "Holt Jacobs, going to the hospital wasn't on the schedule."

I squinted at her, trying to make my brain focus on what was happening. For starters, I was lying on my side while the elf nurse picked glass out of my back, and I no longer had an oxygen mask on. Mom stood over me, and while she'd tried to make a joke about the schedule, there was no hiding how worried she was.

"Sorry," I mumbled. "Juniper made me."

"I did not," Juniper said, and suddenly her head was crowding into view along with Britt's and Dad's. "I tried to get the firemen to load you into my car, but they insisted on the ambulance."

"Blame the firemen," I said so quietly I don't know if they heard.

Then Dad asked someone, "Will he be all right?"

I didn't hear the answer, but it reminded me of the kid. "Wyatt?" I asked the room of faces. "Where's Wyatt?"

"He's okay," Britt said. "They're treating him in another room. He'll be fine."

Wyatt was safe.

"Good," I said and might have smiled.

My room wasn't really big enough for all the medical personnel, plus Britt, Mom, Dad, and Juniper, so my family took turns holding my hand and talking to me. I honestly have no idea what they said, but I'm sure no earth-shattering confessions were made.

Dad and Juniper had just left the room, but instead of Mom and Britt returning, Wyatt walked in.

"Hey," he said, carrying some sort of bundle, with most of his teenage swagger back in place.

"Hey," I said.

Wyatt wandered around my room, not looking at me while not *not* looking at me.

When my elf nurse jingled out of the room, Wyatt went to the closest chair and sat beside me.

"So..." he said, clearly uncomfortable. "I have your stuff." Wyatt handed over my cell phone, then set the bundle on the edge of my hospital bed.

"Is that...my coat?"

"Yeahhh." Wyatt stared at the floor.

Moving slowly with my banged-up ribs, I carefully unfolded the jacket. Tan paint smears showed up in random spots from when Wyatt had climbed onto my shoulders. There were also long tears from the window glass exposing the white insulation in the middle. It was almost funny that this morning I'd been worried about Harper getting glitter glue on this coat.

"Uh...thanks for returning it."

Wyatt rolled his eyes. "Just get a new coat."

"Oh, I plan to." For a moment we both grinned. Then I remembered what Britt had said about him being checked out. "Did it keep you safe?"

Wyatt's brows creased. "Yeah. I'm good. And, uh, thanks."

I shrugged. "Anytime."

Neither one of us had anything more to say, but I was stuck in bed and Wyatt wasn't leaving.

"Oh." Wyatt brightened. "Did you hear what happened to William?"

"No." I half sat up. "Was he waiting for you?"

"Nooo." From Wyatt's tone, I'd regained my spot as a dumb adult. "I called 911 and told them about the fire, and then I explained William started it and he was the one who'd killed Mr. Zeke. Anyway"—Wyatt leaned closer—"you know how he used gasoline for the fire?"

I nodded.

"Well, the cops found him pulled over on the side of the road because he'd run out of gas."

"What!" I said so loudly Britt peeked her head in.

Wyatt didn't see her and kept talking. "Right? He could go on one of those lists of stupid criminals."

"I guess," I said, shaking my head.

Another long silence was threatening, but Wyatt stood. "Anyway"—the bravado almost slipped—"this is probably weird or whatever, but my aunt always says two-dollar bills are lucky, so"—a superhero wallet appeared, and he removed a two-dollar bill and handed it to me—"thank you."

Is this really happening?

I grinned. "I save your life and you give me two dollars?"

"A two-dollar *bill*." Wyatt deflated then. "But yeah, it's dumb. My aunt is...crazy." He tried to take the money back, but I moved my hand away.

"Sorry," I said. "I'm not thinking clearly. This is perfect. Thank you."

"It is?" For a second Wyatt sounded like a little kid.

"Absolutely," I said. "I'll take good care of this."

Wyatt's momentary relief vanished and was replaced with his usual bravado. "Whatever," he said. "It's dumb anyway."

I nodded. "The dumbest."

Wyatt almost laughed but frowned instead. "I should go."

"Wyatt"—I extended my hand—"thanks for getting help."

He froze, then shook my hand and disappeared out the door.

Before I could take a breath, Mom was standing at the entrance. "I asked, and while we're waiting for test results, you can take a shower to scrub off the smoke and paint."

"All right."

A shower was probably for the best since I smelled like an ashtray. But I didn't want to shower. My skin was full of glass cuts, and my ribs preferred it when I stayed still.

The elf nurse reappeared, jingling as she helped me out of bed. I was handed a towel and two mini bottles of baby shampoo and directed to the patient shower. I'd just closed the door when there was a knock. It was Mom. "Here are clean clothes for after."

"Thanks."

I didn't get all the paint off. I didn't get *most* of it off. But I was able to get the smell of smoke out of my nostrils, which was good enough for one night.

Once I was dressed and back in the room, Dad and Juniper were waiting.

"Sorry we forgot you," Dad said, his eyes almost haunted—he'd even forgotten to bring a book.

"Eh," I said, lying back on the bed. "I was around to help Wyatt. It all worked out."

Dad grunted but didn't say anything else. Juniper, on the other hand, was armed with a comb. "Let me get some of the paint out of your hair while it's still wet."

I nodded, because I was too worn out to disagree. Juniper was surprisingly gentle as she worked the comb through my hair. Once I yelped when she reached the tender spot Wyatt had grabbed, but otherwise it went smoothly.

As nice as it was, I wanted Brittany. I looked toward the doorway, where I could see Britt and Mom having a serious conversation with my doctor.

"What's going on?"

"Um"—Juniper made her innocent baby face—"I don't know."

"Juniper?"

She scrunched her nose. "Fine. They're trying to get you home tonight so we can all be together for Christmas."

Huh. I hadn't thought about that. Spending Christmas in the hospital would be pretty depressing.

Juniper continued combing my hair and picking out paint gunk, while Dad sat flexing his fingers and looking everywhere but at me, and we all waited to hear whether I was leaving the hospital tonight.

Mom was smiling when she entered the room, while Britt remained in the hallway with the doctor. "They'll release you," she said. "It's a good thing you're dating a paramedic."

"She's the best," I said.

It still took a long time to actually be released, but finally the elf nurse was pushing me in a wheelchair to my parents' SUV, with Dad and Britt walking on either side of me. I probably didn't need the wheelchair, but I didn't argue when it appeared and the nurse told me to get in.

Britt sat beside me in the middle seat, and Dad drove us back to the lodge, while Mom kept Juniper company in her car. Half the town's Christmas lights were off, and there were only a couple of cars on the road. How late was it?

Leaning against Britt, I tried to relax. "I'm glad you're here."

She squeezed my hand.

As tired as I was, I couldn't sleep. For some reason, the movement of the car left me queasy. We were almost to the house when I leaned forward to watch for the reindeer on fake Santa's roof, the skeptic in me needing to confirm Santa Claus wasn't my next-door neighbor.

Here's the thing. I didn't see the sleigh or the reindeer. Maybe Mr. Claus had turned off the Christmas lights illuminating the reindeer. Or I was too out of it to see them. But half-delirious in the middle of the night on Christmas Eve, I did wonder at the missing reindeer.

Still, not the real Santa.

At the lodge, all the Christmas lights were on. The front door was open before Dad had the car in park. I was slow getting out—my muscles were weirdly stiff.

"We got you," Nigel said, and suddenly he and Jude had their arms wrapped around my shoulders, and they half carried me across the driveway. As we walked up the porch steps, Nigel muttered, "You said not to worry and that everything was fine."

"And your family is safe as promised," I said in a croaky voice.

Nigel stopped walking—I don't think he'd realized he'd made his comment out loud. But since he'd stopped moving, Jude and I were also stopped. It took a long time for Nigel to open his mouth. "Holt"—his voice was very low—"you're a part of my family."

I blinked. That was unexpected.

And Jude's comment of "What he said" left me wondering whether I was dreaming.

"Thanks," I said, because I didn't know what else to say.

There was an awkward pause, where none of us knew what we should do next. Then Jude said, "Let's go," and my brothers-in-law resumed walking me inside.

As nice as it was to be out of the hospital, I'd forgotten about my air mattress in the pantry. Just the act of lying down sounded unpleasant. Thankfully, my brothers-in-law didn't bring me there and instead deposited me on the large recliner in the living room.

Britt took off my shoes so smoothly, I didn't realize what she'd done until after they were off. Next, she was covering me with a thick blanket, before perching on the armrest and smoothing the hair off my forehead.

"How about a Christmas movie?" Casey asked.

For some reason everyone was looking at me. "Sure," I said.

"What movie should we watch?" Juniper asked.

Dad's eyes twinkled. "How about Holt's favorite Christmas movie?"

Casey nodded. "*Die Hard*'s perfect."

Die Hard is a Christmas classic. Problem was, this time I didn't get to enjoy it. John McClane hadn't even left the airplane before I conked out.

CHRISTMAS

A hand was at my throat. I was a little too groggy to react, but when I heard, "Ankle Hold?" I knew I wasn't in danger.

"Hey," I said, my voice extra raspy.

"Did you see Santa?" Baxter's voice held childlike awe.

"Um…" I managed to get my eyelids open. For a moment I thought of the possible missing reindeer on our neighbor's roof, but it was too ridiculous in the light of day, so I said, "No. I must've just missed him."

"Kids," someone called.

Suddenly the room was flooded with adults, and Harper was scooped off my lap. "Sorry, Holt," Casey was saying. "We told them you were sleeping in the living room because you were waiting for Santa. I guess they decided to wake you up and ask."

"It's fine," I said and proceeded to have a gross hacking cough attack.

"Drink this," Britt said, giving me a mug filled with a sweet warm concoction that eased the burning in my throat.

"Since everyone's awake, let's get started," Mom said.

I flopped back against the recliner. Mom had probably let me sleep past whatever time she'd scheduled for gift opening, but she couldn't waste a single minute once I'd woken up. Problem was I felt pretty deathy and at least needed to wash my face and brush my teeth.

"Excuse me."

Getting out of the recliner was a bit of a struggle, and Jude ended up giving me a hand. Once I'd freshened up, I headed to the pantry to get Britt's Christmas present. Juniper caught me in the dining room. "No sneaking off."

I gave her a glare and continued my journey to the pantry. Unsurprisingly, Juniper followed.

"What are you doing?" she asked as I sat on the air mattress and opened up my suitcase. "Come on. You know Mom's waiting."

What was Juniper up to? Before I could consider the question, I experienced another round of coughing that left me nauseated.

"Holt?"

I shook my head. "Would Mom let me skip Christmas?"

"Nope." Juniper sat beside me, making the whole air mattress shift. "You've already missed this year's Mother's Day brunch."

"Hey!" I shoved Juniper's shoulder. "I missed that because I was in the hospital!"

"Mm"—Juniper pursed her lips together—"today you're not in the hospital."

"Whatever," I said. Then I dug to the bottom of my suitcase and retrieved Britt's wrapped present.

"First Christmas together," Juniper said, eyeing the gift. "Did you nail it?"

"Trust me. I nailed it."

"That's good because I don't think she slept at all last night."

"Why?"

"Because of you."

Yes. That was the obvious answer. But I'd almost died last night and hadn't had coffee yet, so I was a little slow connecting the dots.

Juniper shook her head like I was hopeless. "Do you remember anything after the movie started?"

"Nope."

"Here." Juniper began playing a video on her phone. The lighting was dim with lots of shadows, but watchable. There I was wheezing and spluttering. Britt moved me so I was leaning up against her. She rubbed my back, had me drink something, and got me to cough all while saying encouraging things. My replies were nondescript gurgles. Once I'd settled down, she eased me back against the recliner.

Wow.

When the video ended, I slid my finger against the screen, in case there were more. Technically, there was another video, but this one had fire trucks.

"Don't watch that," Juniper said, trying to grab the phone from my hand.

"Juniper?" I asked, holding the phone out of her reach.

The video played. There was plenty of smoke, and then, emerging through the haze, came a firefighter carrying my limp body in a fireman's hold and depositing me on a gurney, which was rushed into an ambulance.

"You filmed that?!"

"I film when I'm nervous." Her face was red. "Please. I didn't even realize it was recording."

I shook my head. "You're unbelievable."

Mom appeared—making us both jump. "And you're both late. Come on. Time for the family picture."

In the time I'd been gone, the rest of the family had been arranged on and around the couch with a corner cushion reserved for me beside Britt.

The whole process took only a couple of minutes and was surprisingly painless. Once Mom had enough family shots, Dad handed me a cup of coffee. Everyone seemed a little off. Like they were part of an inside joke that I didn't know about. Mom and Juniper were especially smug.

I took a few gulps of coffee, then almost did a spit take when I figured it out.

Everyone—including me—was wearing red-and-black plaid pajamas.

"You used me almost dying last night to get me into a pair of matching pj's for your Christmas card!"

"Ah, he figured it out." Juniper literally did a twirl in the living room. "I was scared you were going to your room to change."

I frowned at Britt. "You let them do this?"

Brittany's lips quirked as she held in a smile. "Your mom did ask me to get you to wear them."

"Traitor."

Before anything else could be said on the topic, Harper stood in front of me holding a wrapped gift. "Present?" she asked, handing me the gift.

My frown broke into a smile as Mom and Juniper said, "Aww."

"Thank you, Harper." I took the gift, and since it was addressed to Jude, handed it off when Harper wasn't looking.

Mom let the kids open all their gifts first. As we watched, I took turns drinking coffee and the concoction Britt had given me. I had to drink both. Whatever was in Britt's drink soothed my throat and lungs, but it wasn't coffee. I really love coffee.

Brittany had been sitting beside me, but after opening a particularly fascinating toy, Harper made Britt join her on the floor.

Once Britt was gone, Mom moved to take her spot. She had shadows under her eyes—though actually all the grown-ups looked a little haggard and zombie-ish.

"Did anyone sleep last night?" I asked, quiet enough only Mom heard.

"Oh." She waved her hand like it was nothing. "Most of us got around four hours."

A giggle from Harper brought our attention to where Britt was playing with her. "She didn't sleep. Brittany was by your side all night." Something in Mom's voice—a sad undertone—made me take a closer look.

I cleared my throat, wondering if I'd mess this up. "Thank you for letting her take point."

Mom's cheeks turned pink, and she was uncharacteristically hesitant. Then, tilting her head, she replied, "Thanks for bringing a girlfriend to our family Christmas."

I rolled my eyes. "You're impossible."

Mom smiled. "So are you."

When it was time for the adults to open their presents, it began a longer process of each of us opening a present, then acting all excited and thanking the giver profusely. We weren't even halfway done when I started flagging.

Another coughing attack made my ribs flare up, and my entire body felt like I had the flu. Around this time Mom left and Britt came to sit beside me.

"Just a little bit longer," Britt whispered. I could see the scar by her eyebrow, so I clearly didn't look good. Still, Britt's face wasn't her calm paramedic mask, so overall I was probably fine.

"Your turn," Juniper announced, handing Britt the present from me.

I'd boxed her gift and wrapped it well, but the wrapping paper had gotten a little beat-up in my suitcase and no longer looked fancy.

Britt shook the box, sniffed it, then asked Juniper, "Do you know what this is?"

Juniper shook her head.

"All right." Brittany started tearing the paper, but her eyes were on me instead of the box. Only at the last second did she look away to remove the lid.

Inside the box, a note rested on tissue paper.

"What's it say?" Juniper asked as Britt held the card.

"Handmade by Holt Jacobs." Britt's eyes held mine. There was so much emotion in them, I couldn't understand it all.

I shrugged. "You said your family did handmade gifts."

Britt nodded slowly, then carefully unfolded the tissue paper and gasped.

"What is it?" Juniper was now peering over Britt's shoulder.

"It's..." Britt's eyes were wide as she picked up the hat I'd knit. "This...This is the same shade of purple as..."

"The dress you wore on our first date?" My voice was extra deep. "I remember."

"You learned to knit?" Casey asked, fanning herself.

"Yeah." I shifted in my seat. Having everyone's attention was pretty uncomfortable.

"Was this your first time knitting?" Britt asked, putting on the hat. "It's perfect."

"Well...that hat's actually my third try. The first person I found on YouTube wasn't a good teacher, and I ended up with a bundle of knotted yarn. I found someone better, but when it was done, the hat was all floppy. This one, though, turned out all right."

Britt was touching her head. "I love it."

"Holt's turn," Juniper announced before I could answer Britt.

The gift Juniper handed me was from Brittany.

"Wait!" Brittany's face had gone pale. "Don't open that." The next second she'd snatched the gift from my hands.

"Britt?"

She shook her head. "This isn't a real present. I mean it was...like when I saw it I thought of you, but then you went through all this work to make me something special. And this"—she shook the package—"is more of a gag gift."

What had Britt done?

"Just"—Brittany covered her face with her hand—"let me get you something different."

As curious as I was about the present, I was about to agree. The woman I loved was horrendously uncomfortable on Christmas morning in front of my family after staying up all night watching over me.

As if sensing my answer, Juniper grabbed the present from Britt. "Either Holt opens this or I do."

"Juniper," Mom said, but the admonishment was half-hearted. Apparently everyone wanted to know what was in the package.

"Okay. Whatever," Brittany said. "Give it to him."

Juniper handed me the present while Brittany stared down at the floor.

"Are you sure?" I asked.

Britt wouldn't look at me, but she nodded. Without further ceremony, I tore open the paper. It was a T-shirt. Just a gray T-shirt that said, *I'm fine*, on the front.

"It's great," I said, the words sounding faker than I'd intended.

"Unfold it."

I did as Britt suggested, and a grin spread across my face. "Wow."

"Show it," Casey said.

I held up the shirt. *I'm fine* was written on the chest, but printed along the side were deep reds simulating blood stains.

Someone started applauding, and the rest of the family joined in. Brittany wouldn't look at anyone, but she was no longer slumped over.

"Let me try it on." Unbuttoning the plaid flannel Mom had tricked me into wearing, I pulled the T-shirt over my head, wincing when my ribs objected. "It's soft," I said. "Thank you."

After I kissed her cheek, she looked at me. "You really like it?"

"Yes. It's incredible."

With the mystery solved, Juniper kept the unwrapping going at a quick rate. I'd say she was turning into Mom, trying to keep everyone on schedule, but the real reason was Juniper wanted to know what her presents were as fast as possible.

Finally, it was all done.

The kids moved their new toys into the dining room, where Dad and Nigel worked on assembling a few of them.

Everyone else wandered from the living room, either going upstairs or to the kitchen. Chouzie was left guarding the floor by my feet while I remained on the couch. I'd put the long-sleeved flannel back on because it was warm, but I left it unbuttoned to show off Britt's shirt.

Who knew when Mom's next scheduled event would be, but I'd need a nap before that happened. Problem was, even thinking about sleeping on the air mattress made my ribs ache worse.

"Here." Somehow Brittany had returned without me noticing. She had a fresh mug of her special brew. I took a few sips and felt a little better.

"If only this were hot cocoa," I said.

Brittany half smiled, but her sleepless night was finally showing up on her face.

"Why don't you go lie down?" I suggested. "I promise not to asphyxiate while you're gone."

A faint sparkle lit her eyes, but she shook her head. "No. I'm fine."

"Well, I'm also fine," I said, pointing to my shirt.

"You're always fine," she said.

Britt started to sit beside me, but then she curled her feet up and I stretched my arm out, and one way or another her head was nestled against my uninjured side.

"Careful." My voice was gravelly. "If I'm supposed to stay awake, you'd better do something fast."

Britt's only reply was a faint sigh.

"Britt?"

I couldn't see her eyes, but from the steady rise and fall of her chest, I knew she was already asleep. I couldn't stop my grin. For once I was awake when Brittany was sleeping. But that wouldn't last long. Stretching out my legs on the coffee table, I got better adjusted and closed my eyes. If my only gift from Santa was a Christmas nap with Brittany, I wouldn't complain.

This was shaping up to be one great Christmas.

———— ◄O► ————

What will Holt do at a work conference when one of the attendees wants him dead? Read *A Not So Simple Seminar* to find out!

Ready for a holiday treat? Sign up for my newsletter at *lilystirlin g.com* and receive a copy of the snack-sized mystery, *Holt Jacobs & The Mystery of the Missing Sunglasses*.

Success!

Victory is yours! Not only have you just read an entire book, but you're also full of holiday cheer!

...Or *I hope* you're full of holiday cheer.

No matter how many times I read this book, the ending still makes me want to eat sugar cookies and tell my entire family I love them.

How did the book make you feel? It would really help potential readers if you left a review.

I've wanted to write a Christmas book ever since I was little. Not only do I love Christmas stories, but now all of those Hallmark movies I've watched can be considered *research*.

Montana is beautiful in the winter. The snow-covered mountains mixed with some icy roads made it the perfect setting for Holt's fourth book...though speaking as someone who's slid off the road and landed in a ditch, I believe Holt's suggestion about "Christmas in the desert" is a valid point.

Speaking of deserts, Holt Jacobs's next mystery takes place in Phoenix, Arizona. *A Not So Simple Seminar* occurs during a work retreat—a fun twist for a delightful mystery. I hope you enjoy it!.

If you want to hang out some more, join my newsletter at *lilysti rling.com.* You'll receive every-other-week amusing anecdotes, plus a Holt Jacobs stocking stuffer sized story, *Holt Jacobs & The Mystery of the Missing Sunglasses.*

Thanks for reading!

~ *Lily Stirling*

ABOUT THE AUTHOR

Lily Stirling is the writer of the Holt Jacobs Mystery series.

She has spent a quarter of a century living in the Pacific Northwest. Lily was born in Idaho, but her family moved to Washington around the time she could read chapter books.

Mysteries have always delighted her, from listening to The Hardy Boys on car trips to watching episodes of Psych.

As for sarcastic families, when she's not writing about one, she's living in one.

Acknowledgements

I'm so thankful for everyone on my production team. Thanks for all you do!

Production Team:

Developmental Editor ~ Kristen Weber

Copyeditor ~ Penina Lopez

Proofreader ~ Elaini Caruso

Cover Designer ~ Mariah Sinclair

———◆◯◆———

A huge thanks goes to my family for always making Christmas sparkle with love, laughter, and plenty of good food!

Also, thanks are due to all the adults who volunteered to chaperone ski retreats over New Year's when I was a teen. I truly appreciate it—though I may not have thanked you at the time.

Thanks to Alessandra, Terezia, Eva, and my author friends at Inkers Mastermind. It's been incredible to have such a supportive writing community.

Finally, thank *you* for reading my book and all the back matter. I hope you love *A Not So Cozy Christmas* as much as I do!

Until next time!

Lily Stirling

HOLT JACOBS MYSTERY SERIES

A Not So Shocking Murder
A Not So Rustic Retreat
A Not So Rosy Vintage
A Not So Cozy Christmas
A Not Simple Seminar